WHERE THE EAGLES FLY

SULA BRISTOW

Gary,
This is the most personal gift I can give You — some of my own thoughts and memories!
Merry Christmas!
Your friend and neighbor, Sula

TATE PUBLISHING
AND ENTERPRISES, LLC

Published by Tate Publishing & Enterprises, LLC
127 E. Trade Center Terrace | Mustang, Oklahoma 73064 USA
1.888.361.9473 | www.tatepublishing.com

Tate Publishing is committed to excellence in the publishing industry. The company reflects the philosophy established by the founders, based on Psalm 68:11,
"The Lord gave the word and great was the company of those who published it."

Book design copyright © 2014 by Tate Publishing, LLC. All rights reserved.
Cover design by Allen Jomoc
Interior design by Jomar Ouano

Published in the United States of America

ISBN: 978-1-63306-527-7
Fiction / Family Life
14.08.15

CHAPTER 1

S ax shivered in the cool, autumn night air as he peered angrily through the open cracks of the corn crib. His sun-bleached, straw colored hair was matted and sticky. He flushed again, in humiliation, as he thought of the older boys who had roughed him up and smeared taffy in his hair. His eyes, blue as for-get-me-nots, had clouded, but he hadn't given the bullies the satisfaction of breaking into tears. They had given him a parting shove and taunting laughter as they ran off to find some other mischief. To make it worse, one of the boys had been his brother, Joe.

"If'n ah was oney bigger," he muttered to himself, "ah'd fix 'em good!" He swiped a grubby fist across his eyes to wipe away any tell-tale signs of moisture. "That ole Joe…he's always pickin' on me. Someday ah'll pay him back!"

After the boys had gone, Sax had crawled into the corn crib to hide just in case his tormentors would return. As he burrowed down into the cobs for more warmth, he could hear the lively strains of his father's fiddle and the laughter and banter of the dancers in the new barn. The day had been full of fun and excitement until those boys had ruined it for him. He dragged his mind from them and let it relive the earlier events before falling into a tired sleep.

＊ ＝◆＝ ＊

The day had begun earlier than usual; when Martha Saxon had bustled into the children's bedroom, tousling a head here, and yanking a cover there. "Up! You sleepy heads!" she had called them gaily. "We have a barn raisin' to go to."

Crocketts, who lived a few miles away, had lost their barn to a fire. Their house had been spared. "Thanks to the good Lord," Sax's mother said. Neighbors for miles around were putting aside their own work to congregate at Crocketts to erect a new barn before bad weather set in.

John Saxon was home, too. The children felt varying degrees of pleasure and apprehension. They saw him so seldom that they never knew how he was going to accept their behavior. They did not have the warm relationship with him which they did with their mother.

John was a teamster who hauled freight, by mule team from St. Louis or Kansas City, to communities that still had no railroads. He, therefore, was gone a good deal of the time. He was a man of medium build, sporting a mustache, blue eyes, and an already receding hairline; he had an unpredictable temper at times.

Although the hour was early, the Saxons were not the first to arrive at Crocketts. There was already a buzz of activity and conversation in progress, with more arrivals continually until it seemed that everyone in the county had turned out. The women had each brought some delicious dish of food, which they felt special pride in preparing, for the common meal to be shared later. Long tables made from saw horses and boards were soon groaning under the weight of the tempting food. Clean sheets were spread over the top to keep dust and insects away until time to eat.

While the men and older boys worked on the barn, the women and adolescent girls visited while working on a quilt. The younger children had a grand time playing with friends that were seldom seen. A hodgepodge of color, sounds, and scents had assailed Sax. He was enthralled with all the activity; his inquisitive eyes darting around trying to take in everything at once. He had played for a while but soon drifted over to watch the progress on the barn.

Always interested in how things were built or put together, he was never tired of watching and had a grasp of things beyond his years. He sniffed eagerly, enjoying the pungent odor of freshly cut boards and the bustle of activity around him.

The barn took form so quickly that it almost seemed magical to Sax. Saxon had cautioned his young son sharply several times and finally ordered him back in no uncertain terms. "Don't git under foot!"

Sax had moved back but found a vantage point on the rail of a nearby fence, where he could watch the progress without further reprimands. He liked to listen to the men talk, too. It was giving him a feeling of being involved in something important, even if he didn't understand it all. He often heard references to a war which was recently over and was a little frightened because there was so much anger and bitterness in some of the voices.

"Things were bad enough before the war," one lean fellow with blazing eyes said, "but now they're worse! The border raids along Kansas are still out of hand and the slave issue ain't settled by a damn sight!"

Others had joined in the heated debate until the talk turned to the James gang, run by the notorious brothers, Jesse and Frank. Frank was the elder, but Jesse seemed to be the undisputed leader. This subject, too, brought on a hot argument.

"They oughta be caught and hung!" said the dark-featured man.

Another gaunt farmer replied, "Hell, no. They deserve a medal! They was drove tuh do what they're doin'. Their family was treated real bad."

"They shoulda been...the damned southern sympathizers," another angry voice proclaimed.

"Well, regardless," someone changed the subject. "Things are gittin' so bad around here, I think one o' these days I'm just gonna pull up stakes and go west."

Others agreed, "Why not git in on some o' that gold that's just layin' around fer the takin'!"

Sax was a little surprised and excited to hear his father's voice join eagerly in this discussion but also noticed his older brother Sam with an angry glower on his face.

"That's fer me!" John had said. "I've been as far as Santa Fe before."

Another burly fellow announced firmly, "Yuh cain't believe everthin' yuh hear."

"No, but when there's smoke, there's fire. There must be some truth to all these stories of people gettin' rich!"

"Yeah, unless it's like those crazy stories a few years back, what come out in the papers even! I recollect they claimed Pike's Peak was a solid mass o' gold! Said they'd come up with a real easy way tuh dig it. All they had tuh do was toboggan down the slopes on a sled with sharp iron runners. Said that'd scrape off a thin layer o' gold, curlin' it like wood shavin's. Then all they was sposed tuh have tuh do was sweep up the gold curls by the ton after each toboggan ride!"

Loud guffaws followed this story, but one die-hard said, "I still say there be some truth to all the tales of fortunes made out there."

Sax listened eagerly to this exciting banter and was a little disappointed when talk turned to more mundane things. He day-dreamed a little, wondering what it would be like to go west and find gold and become rich. Not that he knew what *rich* meant. He just liked the sound of it. And it sure seemed to be what the men wanted, his father included.

The barn had gone together in record time, so before night fall it was completed. They had eaten at noon, but there was plenty of food left for the evening meal. Then it was taken for granted there was to be music and dancing in the traditional barn warming.

Parties were few and far between for these hardworking families, so they took advantage of the opportunity to extend this time of fellowship and fun.

"Where's your fiddle, John?" someone called to Sax's father. "Can't have a good hoe-down 'thout a fiddle!"

"Hey, Mose," another voice joined in, "git out your mouth organ. Yeah…and Pete, drag out that old squeeze box. We're fixin' tuh have us a dance, by golly!"

Sax saw his mother swung out onto the floor, her cheeks flushed, eyes sparkling, and curly tendrils of chestnut hair escaping from the braid that circled her small head. He thought she had never looked prettier.

Some of the young people organized a taffy pull while the smaller ones played hide-and-seek. That was when some of the boys decided to liven things up, and Sax wound up with taffy in his hair and everywhere else they had been able to smear him. It wasn't until the party was winding down and mothers started gathering up tired and sleeping children, that Martha missed Sax. Her brows drew together in a worried frown as her deep gray eyes darted here and there, seeking her five-year-old.

"Lucy, when did you see Sax last?" she asked her daughter.

"Not since they was makin' taffy, Mama. "And some of the boys was pickin' on him, too!" she added indignantly. Sax was her favorite brother and since she was only two years older, they spent much time together and got along especially well.

Martha hurried over to the wagon, where John was hitching up the team and explained the situation to him.

He quickly collared Joe and demanded an explanation, asking if he had been the instigator of Sax's harassment.

The boy ducked his head sheepishly. "Not exactly, Pa, but—"

"But what?" John Saxon's blue eyes were blazing and his slight form was ramrod stiff. He seemed much taller than his actual height to his twelve-year-old son, who knew he better have the right answers. He shuffled his feet nervously and cleared his suddenly dry throat.

"I didn't start it, but…but I didn't stop it, either." He stared at his toe, making aimless circles in the dirt. "I was there. I'm sorry, Pa. Honest"

"You're gonna be a lot sorrier, son, but ah'll deal with you later. Now, we have tuh find Sax. Where was all this goin' on?"

Joe pointed toward some sheds and outbuildings, some distance from the barn. His father headed in that direction calling over his shoulder, "You boys scour the area around here and look for your little brother. Ah'll start over this way."

Martha put Lucy in charge of her sleeping two-year-old Elsa and went to help look for Sax. The Crocketts and neighbors, who hadn't yet left, joined in the search. Martha understood her little son quite well. She knew that he had a temper and a very stubborn streak at times. She also realized that he would have deeply resented the treatment of the older boys. She wondered what his reaction would have been. Would he have run? Cried? Hid? She decided it would have been the latter. Sax rarely cried. He didn't want to be considered a baby. She started looking for good hiding places and softly calling to him, "Sax, honey, it's Mama. Won't you come out now? It's time to go home."

She could hear the other voices in the distance, calling, too. Deep men's voices and the higher pitched women's and children's. Crocketts' dog had been running after first one and then another, wondering what all the excitement was about. He was prancing around Martha's feet as if it were some grand new game they were playing, when he stopped suddenly, pricking his ears and then running over to the corn crib. He started barking insistently. Martha went to the crib, calling to Sax all the while. She tried to peer over the top from her scant five feet, but was unable, so she climbed up on the slats, looking into the darkness below. There came a muffled whimper and sudden movement of dislodged corn cobs as Sax sat up. "Mama, is that you?"

"Yes, honey, come to Mama. We're goin' home." She wrapped her arms around the boy, as he climbed over the rail. "Thank the good Lord you're alright!"

"John!" she called. "I've found him. He's safe!"

To Sax, she whispered. "You really scared the livin' daylights out of us…don't ever do that again."

"But they wouldn't let me have any taffy, an' they was mean an' stuck it in muh hair an' knocked me down! Ah hate 'em! Ah wisht ah was big 'nuff tuh git even!"

Martha gently soothed the boy, and they were soon on their way home. He was a mess that required some cleaning up before bed, late as it was. She had to clip away tufts of hair that were so matted with taffy, dirt, and bits of corn husks, that it was impossible to get a comb through. The rest of his body was an equally grubby sight. Much as he grumbled about being bathed, he felt good afterward, and snuggled under the bedcovers with a happier feeling than he'd had in a good many hours.

CHAPTER 2

John had dealt with Joe in a manner that left the boy relieved to have his father take off for another freight trip. John was going to Kansas City this time or Westport, as he still thought of it.

"The name was good enough before. Don't know why they wanted tuh change it," he grumbled.

Missouri had been known as the gateway to the west for a long time; first, for the fur traders, then for forty-niners and settlers heading to Oregon, California, and Texas. St. Louis had been founded as a fur trading post by the French in the 1700s and had become a prosperous town. The American flag had been raised there in 1804. After that time, furs from the Rockies came to St. Louis, Westport and other river towns by the overland trade with Santa Fe.

This trade was chiefly by individual adventurers who outfitted at these river towns, which had become supply centers. They brought the gold and silver bullion, furs, and horses, then on the return trip hauled manufactured goods, textiles, and such things that were eagerly wanted by the settlers farther west. They rendezvoused for an annual caravan, as individuals and small groups suffered severely from Indian attacks. Attacks were seldom made on the larger caravans.

With the gold rush to California, overland traffic increased dramatically. St. Louis became the main supply center. Goods were transported from there to Kansas City and St. Joseph by steamboat. From these towns it was taken elsewhere by ox and mule teams. John Saxon was one of these freighters. He had, however, gone with one of the caravans, as a driver, to Santa Fe, when he was unmarried. The trip had been a memorable adventure for him. He yearned to go again.

He remembered the brief encounter with the renegade Indian, Buzzard Wing, and his rag-tag group of followers. They had not attacked the wagons, as it had been too large a group for them to attempt it. Rather, they had harassed it, staying just out of rifle range, making obscene and threatening gestures. John had been told it was always so with the larger groups, but smaller ones were attacked; wagons looted and burned and people killed.

"They say he carried off a white woman one time, making her his squaw."

John often thought of these things. He wondered who the poor woman had been. Remembering the dark, leering visage of Buzzard Wing, he had no doubt about the story being true.

John thought of his wife. Martha was a good woman. A pretty one, too, in spite of the hard work and childbearing that had been her lot. However, being away so much, John had not remained faithful, taking his pleasure where he could find it. His guilt made him less comfortable around Martha each time he was home. Much as he tried to find something to fault her for, he had no doubt of her faithfulness to him. As a consequence, he spent more time away and less at home as time went by.

The children, too, were a sore spot. They were almost strangers, the older ones treating him with polite but restrained behavior and the little ones avoiding him shyly. Only Sax acted as if he was unafraid of his father, but somehow John couldn't warm up to the boy. He wondered why. Was it because Sax wasn't afraid of him? John shook his head ruefully. He pushed such thoughts out of his mind. *After all*, he thought, half angrily, *a man's gotta make a livin'.*

When the suspicion of a doubt entered his mind, with the thought, that most men made their living near their families, John dismissed it with head thrown back and jaw outthrust.

It was a time of unrest and dissension in Missouri, as the men at the barn-raising had indicated. The slavery issue and the Civil War had engendered bitter hatred. The border raids along Kansas had long been fomenting unrest. The conflict had raged there for seven years before the war, over slavery. Ownership of slaves was legal in Missouri. Would so-called *free* Kansas, right next door, allow slavery when it became a state? Northerners, who opposed ownership of slaves, had settled in Kansas. People from slave states lived in

Missouri, and even though most weren't slave-owners, they felt it was right.

Missourians voted illegally in Kansas, trying to swing the state to slavery. Kansans crept into Missouri and burned and robbed; all convinced that they were in the right. These border raids went on for many years, causing hatred on both sides. The Constitutional Convention of 1865 abolished slavery, but not the hot emotions connected to it.

During these tumultuous years, the James boys had taken up the outlaw life. John knew more than he usually indicated about the Jameses family. His wife had grown up near the family and was a friend of the boys, especially Jesse, being the same age. Jesse's stepfather, Dr. Samuels, had treated Martha's father when he had been badly injured in an accident. Her sister, Sarah, still lived in the vicinity of the Samuels, and sometimes mentioned them in her letters.

Martha had told John that Frank James was a quiet boy who loved books. Jesse, she had indicated, was more of a daredevil, but still soft-spoken and caring, as a boy. The family had come from Kentucky, though, and was naturally sympathetic to the south during the war.

Frank had joined the Confederate side when the war started. Later, he joined up with the notorious William Clarke Quantrill, as did some of the Younger boys, who were now members of the James gang. Jesse was accused of riding with the dreaded Quantrill's Raiders, but in actual fact, when he tried to join them, he was refused because he was too young. He did, however, later join another group under "Bloody" Bill

Anderson. He gained considerable reputation for his marksmanship and daring.

John recalled Martha relating events that led to Jesse's joining Anderson's group.

"It was almost too horrible to tell," she had wept. "It was the summer of 1863. Jesse's folks were known to sympathize with the Confederates. They'd never tried to hide that. And the Union army knew Frank had joined Quantrill's outfit. One day a bunch of Union soldiers rode out to Samuels cabin.

"We want you," they said to the doctor. "We're gonna teach you a lesson!"

They tied his hands behind his back and put a rope around his neck and threw it over a tree limb. They pulled him off his feet and rode off with him danglin' and chokin' somethin' fierce."

Martha had paused, wiping her eyes, and gathering her memories, then spoke again.

"Mrs. Samuels had been workin' 'round back of the house, when she heard the noise. She ran to see what it was just in time to see the soldiers ridin' away and her husband chokin'. By the time she was able to get him down, he was unconscious. Wouldn't have been long 'til he was dead." Martha shuddered slightly before continuing.

"Jesse was out in a field workin'. The soldiers found him, too, and caught him. They whipped him terrible, 'til his back and shoulders was all bloody awful! He was laid up for days. When he was well again, he tried to join Quantrill, but he was too young."

"Another time," she had continued, "when Dr. Samuels and Jesse were gone, the soldiers came again. They arrested Mrs. Samuels and kept her locked up for two weeks before they let her go. It wasn't long after that, Jesse joined up with Anderson."

Saxon pondered these things, thinking that it was no wonder Jesse had learned to hate the north. Some of the others in the James gang had similar experiences. Cole Younger's father had been robbed and killed. A little later, his mother was forced by Union troops to burn her own home. Then they left her stranded, in mid-winter, eight miles from the nearest shelter. She'd had to struggle through deep snow with her four youngest children, to refuge.

These things embittered Cole Younger, even more than he already was, and he took part in Quantrill's bloody raid on Lawrence, Kansas, where the order was to kill every man and burn every house.

John pulled his thoughts back to Jesse James and his plummet to lawlessness. Martha's sister had written in one of her letters, "I know how close you and Jesse were when we were growing up, so it pains me to tell you about his latest troubles. When the terrible war ended, Jesse and some of his companions rode to a school house to surrender, but before they could, they were attacked by Union soldiers. Jesse was hurt very bad. He was shot in the right side of his chest twice and also in the leg. He was close to death for months. He's still not well, but the Samuels are taking him and moving to Nebraska. I don't know if we will see him or his dear parents again."

It had been quite some time before Martha had heard from Sarah again. There had once again been news of Jesse.

"The Samuels have come back from Nebraska, bringing Jesse with them. Mrs. Samuels told me that he had asked them to bring him home, as he didn't want to die in Northern territory. I guess they missed their home, too. When I went to see them, Jesse was still not well, but he had his old puckish nature back. He asked me about you and said, with a grin, "Since Martha's happily married; I have decided who my wife will be. On the way home, I met my cousin, Zee, and have decided that one day she will be my wife.

He went on to tell me that she was named for his mother, Zerelda, but they call her Zee. He said that both of their folks were upset about the thought of them marrying but just wait and see."

Sarah's letter had gone on, "You may have heard that Jesse was with the gang who robbed the Liberty bank. That just isn't so! He was still recuperating from his infected wounds. I suppose you have heard that a young man was killed at the time of that hold-up. He was a completely innocent fellow who happened to be on the street. I think Frank was there, but who can say who did the shooting?

Soon the Saxons had heard, from rumors and reward posters, that Jesse was riding with the gang and had a price on his head. He was now acknowledged as the leader. He rode with a reckless audacity. A story was told, with humor, about a robbery in Iowa. The gang rode into town, unrecognized, while a political speech was going on in the town square. They robbed the bank of $40,000. On the way out of town, Jesse impudently interrupted the speech, unrecognized, and told them there was trouble at the bank. Investigating, they found two men tied up in the back room, and the money all gone.

The next direct news of Jesse was from the outlaw himself. John had been away, as he so often was. Jesse's horse had stumbled in a gopher's hole, on one of his swift night rides. It broke its leg and had to be destroyed. This happened near the Saxon's home. Martha had been awakened by a gentle but persistent tapping at her kitchen door.

Throwing a shawl around her shoulders, she had made her way to the door, calling softly, "Who's there this time of night?'

She heard her name called, assuring her it was someone known to her, although the voice was muffled. Lighting a lamp, she opened the door and was startled to see her old childhood friend standing before her. Mixed emotions played across her face as she gazed at him. His face was leaner, harsher, but he had the same wide smile and thick, dark sandy hair she remembered.

"Martha, I won't blame you if you tell me to get out, but I was taking a chance you might help me." He looked at her intently. "You haven't really changed much," he told her, "still as pretty as ever. But I'm afraid I have changed…all for the worse. Well, at least, let us talk for a few minutes since I'm here. It's been a long time."

She insisted he sit and rest a bit while she fixed coffee and a quick meal. "Sarah has sometimes written of you and your folks," she told him. "I was truly sorry to hear about all your troubles. She said you were thinking of getting married. Did you?"

"Yeah, I married my cousin, Zee. You should have seen the hullabaloo that caused!" he said, with a grin. "Her Uncle Will really had a fit, but he's a minister, you know. Anyway, he finally came around enough to tie the knot for us!"

He chuckled, remembering. "Frank got married, too. Guess it wasn't really fair of us to put wives through this, but they are good and loyal women."

He was silent for a moment, then spoke bitterly, "Guess what really put the spurs to the old devil that's been ridin' me was what they did to my mother and little brother!"

Martha acknowledged she hadn't heard about it, so, over coffee, while he ate, she listened to the sad story.

"The Pinkerton detectives decided that I was holed up at the folks'. They didn't bother to find out for sure but surrounded the house. Then somebody threw something in the window that exploded. It blew my mother's arm off at the elbow, and little Archie, my half-brother…was hurt so bad, he didn't live through the night. And Jenny…the old colored lady that helped out…she was hurt real bad, too."

Martha's eyes brimmed with tears, hearing about her old friends. "I'm so sorry, Jesse." She squeezed his hand." I do so wish things could have been different for you."

"Well, it's too late now…what with a price on my head and everything. I've tried to go straight different times. Took a different name and was going to farm or raise horses. Somebody always recognized me and turned me in as an outlaw. Always had to run…I'd better be going. You don't have a horse you could sell me, do you?"

"All we have's a team, besides the mules John uses for freighting. The team can be ridden, but they're not too fast, you know. But if it will help, you can take one."

"Any's better than none. If any body asks, tell them a horse buyer by the name of Howard bought it. I will see that you get another horse as soon as possible," Jesse told her, "and I won't forget your kindness."

He had gone as quietly as he had arrived. About a month later, a lean, sun-browned stranger had stopped at the Saxon place, leading a pair of beautiful chestnut mares.

"These are from a friend," he told Martha. "A certain Mr. Howard." With a tip of his hat, he had galloped off.

John had questioned her about the horses. Somewhat to his surprise, she had refused to tell him until he gave his word not to tell anyone else. In spite of his other failings, John Saxon tried to be a man of his word. Since his sympathies were also with the James boys, he applauded his wife's actions.

Jesse still had many admirers. Many down-and-out people claimed to have been helped by his generosity. All kinds of legends and stories had sprung up about his exploits. They were even starting to be written up in the popular dime novels. He was becoming larger than life.

CHAPTER 3

The autumn days were happy ones for Sax. He was alone with his mother and small sister, Elsa, much of the time. His older brothers and Lucy were in school. Since his father was away, too, Martha was extremely busy, getting ready for winter. Sax was required to entertain Elsa much of the time. He didn't mind. She was a loving child, toddling after him happily, trying to do what he did, or simply sitting watching him, with thumb jabbed in her rosebud mouth.

Martha had worked tirelessly, gathering garden produce. Root vegetables had been stored in the dugout cellar. She had also packed apples in layers of straw in barrels, with Sax's help, and stored them in the cellar, also. Some apples had been sliced and dried, along with beans and corn. A variety of jams and jellies had been made.

The boy was an interested observer in all these activities. His sponge-like mind absorbed and stored many details without his being aware of it. He laughed when his mother had called the dried green beans *leather britches*, thinking that was a silly thing to call beans.

Martha heaved a satisfied sigh over these chores. "It gives a body a good feelin' to know there's goin' to be enough to eat, come winter." She smiled at Sax.

"Now, soon as I get my kraut put down in crocks, we're goin' to make us some soap. I'm gettin' low, and you youngsters sure do dirty your share of clothes!"

Sax knew that his mother had been saving a supply of wood ashes to make lye, which was needed for the soap. He was curious to see how she would do it. He knew she had made soap last year, but somehow hadn't watched.

The day which Martha designated as soap-making day happened to be a Saturday. The older children were home from school. She assigned chores to them.

"Sam and Joe, you still have wood to cut and stack. We'll need a lot more for winter. And Lucy, you can keep an eye on Elsa and do some of the light chores in the house. Sax is goin' to help me, soon as he feeds the chickens."

Sax grinned happily. His mother hadn't forgotten that he wanted to learn how to make soap. He fairly flew out to tend to the chickens while Martha put a pot of beans on the stove to simmer for their supper. She instructed Lucy to add some water once in awhile so they wouldn't burn. "If you have any trouble with anything, call me," she added, as she left the house.

Walking toward the barn, she beckoned Sax to join her. "We need a hopper to make the lye in," she explained. "My old one is out here."

She proceeded to throw aside some boards and trash to drag out a rough board hopper. Sax thought it looked like a manger or crib. It was a crudely made, trough-shaped hopper, obviously made by Martha, herself. Rough wooden slats formed the sides and the bottom, or trough (made with two boards nailed into a V), which sloped slightly down and extended several inches beyond the end wall of the hopper.

"That," she told her son, "is for the lye to drain down. Now, we need to get us some corn shucks to line it with, so the ashes won't go through the cracks."

They gathered up an arm full from the corn crib, taking them to the hopper. She showed the boy how to spread them over the bottom and side until the cracks were well covered.

"Now, while I get the ashes," Martha said, "you run to the house and get my old enamel bucket to catch the lye in, when it drips off the ashes."

She had put the hopper beside the container holding the wood ashes for this purpose. Uncovering them, she proceeded to shovel them into the hopper until it was within a couple of inches of the top. Sax came running with the bucket, which his mother had him set under the trough spout. "We have to have water now." she explained, "because the water draws the lye out o' the ashes."

They brought water from the well and she poured it over the ashes, slowly and carefully. "Pretty soon it will come drippin' down the trough into the bucket. You have to be careful then, 'cause straight lye is mighty strong…burns bad if it gets on you! So I don't want you touchin' this any more…just watch!"

She added a little more water at intervals, and soon the lye was draining into the bucket, looking like slightly discolored water. "It will be awhile before I have enough for soap," Martha told the boy. "In the meantime, I have to get out my old iron kettle and my grease, and start a fire out here to cook my soap on."

He helped her gather up these items, then watched as she laid the wood for a fire in a little pit in the ground, surrounded by flat stones on which to set the kettle.

When the woman felt she had enough lye, she put part of it in the kettle and added the grease, which she had saved from cooking. She set the kettle over the fire and started stirring the mixture carefully with a huge, long-handled wooden spoon.

"You hafta boil this down until it thickens good. Starts to look like gravy", she explained to Sax. "I could've used my big iron wash-pot, but when you make a great big batch all at once, it don't get hard 'nuff to make bars. Some folks like it soft, but you gotta have somethin' to store it in, then. I like bars. They're easy to store."

She paused while she stirred again, and then continued, just as if she were explaining to an adult. "You can use any kind of grease…leftover, like this, or lard, or mutton tallow. Any kind you have. It all works."

She smiled. "Who knows? Maybe knowin' how to do this will come in handy for you some day."

"Wal, ah jist wondered how." It was his only response.

"Look! It's gettin' right thick now," Martha murmured. "Run and get me some o' them flat wood crates over by the house. We'll pour it in them to harden pretty soon."

While Sax was doing that, she took a handful of dry leaves from her apron pocket and tossed them, crumbled into the kettle. He came back in time to see her stirring them in, so asked about it.

"It's dried mint leaves," she told him. "Soap don't hafta have it, but it adds a nice smell. I usually make some with scent and some without." She added, after a moment, "You can use other things, instead of mint, if you want to."

Looking in the pot again, she observed, "Now, I think it's time to pour it out. You put some corn shucks in the bottom o' these crates."

She picked up the kettle with some thick pads. It was heavy and all she could manage, but she warned Sax to stay back, so he wouldn't get burned. She poured the mixture into the boxes until it was about two inches thick, explaining that it would be allowed to harden overnight before being cut into bars of a convenient size.

"But Mama," asked Sax. If the lye is so strong an' will burn ya so bad, won't the soap burn ya, too?"

Martha laughed merrily. "Have you ever been burned with the soap I wash you with?"

"No, but…" he started to protest.

"The grease some way takes the burnin' out o' the lye when it turns to soap," she said. "I can't tell you exactly how. It just does."

This seemed to satisfy the boy. Martha was glad because it was the best explanation she could give him.

They made several more batches of soap, until she was satisfied that she had enough to last for several months. Then the crates were stacked in a little shed attached to the house. The hopper was emptied and dragged back by the barn, the fire put out and the utensils put away. Martha heaved a sigh of relief at another major chore done.

There was not time to sit back and relax, however. A cold, crisp Saturday in November was to be butchering day. John Saxon was home again and the children were out of school to help. Lucy was in charge of Elsa, and indeed, preferred to stay inside where it was warm.

At an early hour the water was heated to the scalding point in the huge iron wash kettle, which Martha used to do the laundry. While the water was heating, John was killing the hogs. They had three to butcher this year, raised from little pigs. He dispatched them quickly with well-placed shots. The jugular vein was then cut to allow them to bleed.

They were dragged over to the cauldron where they were to be scalded to loosen the coarse hair and bristles, so they could be scraped off with a knife. A kind of scaffold had been constructed over this area, with a long, stout pole, set in forked supports on each end so a hog could be hoisted up, and raised and lowered into the water as needed. They couldn't be left in the water too long or the bristles would anchor more firmly, rather than loosen. Even Sax was allowed to try and scrape off bristles so he could see how it was done.

When one had been scraped clean, the hamstring on each hind leg was exposed, and a short, stout stick, sharpened on both ends, was inserted through the tendons. The hog was strung over the end of the hoisting pole on the end opposite the scalding pot.

The next hog was hauled into position to be scalded. While Martha, Sam, and Joe worked on this, John began the disemboweling process on the first animal. This was done very carefully, as nothing edible was to be wasted. A long cut was made from the crotch to the neck, but not through the membrane holding the entrails. Then he cut the large intestine at the anus and pulled the end free, tying it with a piece of string. He then cut the gullet and sliced the membrane holding the intestines, letting them fall into a tub, placed to catch them. The neck was cut completely around to the backbone at the base of the head. Then it was twisted off and set aside to be used for headcheese or scrapple.

Martha had also provided various pots and pans for other purposes, such as soaking the liver. The kidneys and heart were also saved. The small intestines were salvaged, drained, washed, and set aside to soak, while the butchering continued.

This was an era when it was taken for granted that animals were to be slaughtered for food. The youngsters took this all matter-of-factly. They knew that any animals were kept for food, with the exception of those that earned their keep in other ways, such as horses, milk cows, dogs and cats. It was also a time when it was understood that nothing was wasted. Things were not to be killed wantonly, but when they were slaughtered, they were to be utilized to the fullest.

The fat which held the intestines was cut out and tossed in a bucket to be used for lard. The carcass would be cut up after all were ready. By the time the three animals were at this stage, the family was ready for a break and something to eat.

Martha took a chunk of liver in with her to prepare. It needed to be used first and some of it would make a good quick meal. It had been soaking, so she rinsed it again and sliced it thinly, dipped it in seasoned flour and fried it in bacon fat. Served with onions and fried potatoes, it made a satisfying meal. Replete and warmed, they went back to their work with renewed vigor.

The carcasses were thoroughly washed out, then one by one, were taken to a rough, but sturdy table, built to be used in butchering. John cut the meat into hams, bacon sides, etc. The ribs and backbone were trimmed into small pieces to be canned. Martha trimmed where necessary, throwing excess fat into the lard buckets and lean scraps into the sausage pans.

Sax was a bit overwhelmed by all the meat and pans of odds and ends. He asked his mother what they were going to do with all of it.

"Well, it has to last for a long time so we gotta take care of it so it won't spoil. The ham an' bacon an' such… we'll salt down an' hang in the smokehouse with a little ole fire kept goin', probably hickory or apple wood…to keep smoke goin' up over the meat. That cures it so it'll keep a long time.

The liver an' heart an' such, we have to use up first while we can keep it fresh. Now the little ole intestines there…see, they're cleaned up real good—an' I use them for sausage casin's. You know; I fill them full of sausage after I get it made, an' then I tie it off ever' three or four inches. Then, it's hung in the smokehouse, too. We cut off however many we want at a time…" She worked on as she talked to her son, explaining the process of preserving their winter's meat.

"Now some folks use that little intestine cooked, an' calls 'em chitlins. They cut it up in little pieces an' soak it in salt water for three or four days. Then they wash 'em real good an' dip in batter an' fry'em."

Sax was looking at the heads of the animals, which seemed to be looking back at him. "Are yuh goin' tuh keep them, even?" he asked a bit warily.

"Yes, indeedy!" she replied with her gentle smile. "I know they don't look like much now, but when they're soaked good an' then cleaned and cooked 'til all the meat falls off the bone, it makes real good scrapple. You gotta make sure there's no little bones left in the meat, an' then add sage an' other seasonings. Then throw in some corn meal to make it thick. Then you pour it in some kind of flat pans an' let it set. You can slice it an' fry it then."

It was several days before Martha had all her chores, connected with the butchering, done. Finally, the sausage was all made, the lard rendered and stored in tin buckets, the scrapple made, the canning done and the meat hanging in the smokehouse. She was tired but pleased. It would be a good winter.

CHAPTER 4

It was a good winter, and it passed quickly for Martha. It was her time to relax a bit from her labors. It's not that she wasn't busy. There was always cooking, washing, cleaning, or other household duties to be done. Now, however, she could sit quietly, at times, sewing or knitting or doing a bit of embroidery.

Winter, also, was when John was home more often. Weather, being bad much of the time, brought much of the freight business to a crawl. Known to be handy at carpentry, he was often called on during these slack times to build or repair things for those less adept.

Martha was not ignorant of the fact that John's thoughts were often elsewhere. She saw a certain look come over him as he gazed westward sometimes, when he was unaware that she was watching. She couldn't help wondering if the time would come when he wouldn't return from one of his freight trips. She hoped she was wrong, but she was aware that, through the years, his feelings for her had changed. He tried to be considerate, but it was like an invisible wall had risen between them. He seemed distant even when he was there.

She told herself she was just being foolish and tried to content herself in just having him home. After all, they had been married a long time. She couldn't expect him to feel the same as years ago, could she? Then, all too soon, the weather had warmed and it was time for another freight run, and he was gone again.

The next time he returned it was with an ultimatum. He had decided, he told her, that they were going west to a new life in a new country. *Either go with me, or I'm goin' alone* was his verdict.

Martha's fears had half come true and now she didn't know which was more frightening. Having to pack up and go along or having him leave her and the children behind for good. However, there really was no choice, as far as Martha was concerned. John was her husband. They would go.

"We're gonna hafta hurry," he told her, "tuh make it to St. Joe before the next wagon train leaves. An' there's a lot tuh be done! Ah'll get busy an' try an' sell everythin' we cain't take. You all get busy an' pack what we kin take. Remember…don't take nothin' that ain't absolutely necessary!"

Martha was in a quandary. What to take? Things she had considered necessary in her home would now be superfluous in a wagon, camping along a trail for hundreds of miles. She hardly knew where to begin and yet she must hurry!

The older children were confused and the younger ones excited at the prospect. Sam became balky.

"Ah don't want tuh go west! Nothin' out there but a bunch of dirty savages an' crazy people thinkin' they're gonna get rich! Ah want to stay here. Ole man Jackson promised me a job. He thinks ah'm old enough to do a man's work. Ah'm sixteen next month. Mama, you were hardly older when you got married! Let me stay!"

Martha didn't want her family split up, but John settled the issue. "The boy's right. He's growin' up; practically a man. Let him stay! He'll be better off workin' for Jackson than complainin' all the way to Colorado!"

Joe's objections were brushed aside. "Y'all are goin' an' that's final! Ah don't want to hear another word about it!"

Martha hid her tears to the best of her ability and told Sam she would write as often as she could, and obtained his promise to do likewise as soon as he knew where to send it. He told his family good-bye and went to join the Jackson's.

Martha continued her packing, choosing as wisely as she could. She concentrated mainly on food, bedding and as few cooking utensils as she thought she could get by with.

"What about our cow an' chickens?" she asked her husband.

"We'll try tuh take the cow. If she makes it, she might be worth her weight in gold! You can take a dozen hens an' one rooster. Ah'll make a couple little cages for 'em that we can hang on the side of the wagon.

When we get to St. Joe we're gonna trade wagons. My freight wagon can be used but the little farm wagon you'll be drivin' will have to go. Ain't heavy duty 'nuff."

The trip to St. Joe gave Martha a little foretaste of what lay ahead on the journey to the Shining Mountains, as the Rockies were referred to. She prayed she would be able to endure.

St. Joe was a revelation to Sax and his sisters. He was amazed at all the people. He hadn't known there were that many people in the whole world!

Men from just about every race were represented. Gentlemen, dressed in fine suits, brushed shoulders with mountain men, dressed in buckskins, which wore wicked looking knives strapped around their waists, and carried long rifles. Glistening black men, Chinese, with long pigtails hanging down their backs, wearing funny little round hats, and soldiers of all ranks and descriptions were in the throng filling the streets. Some farmers and their wives, in simple homespun clothing, were gathering supplies for their journey.

They all wanted to go west. It was easy to see why this was called one of the jumping off places. Everyone seemed waiting to jump off to somewhere else.

As they reached the far side of town, near the river, dozens of covered wagons and camp fires came into view. This was where the wagon train was forming. Some of them had spent the winter here, waiting for the weather to warm up enough to start out. Some, like Saxon's, had just arrived, and others had been here for a short time, waiting for relatives to join them to make the trek together.

John was impatient to start making inquiries about getting another wagon and oxen or mules to pull it. Also, to check with some knowledgeable person about just what supplies were deemed necessary for the journey? He hardly took time to unhitch his mules and the chestnut mares before leaving on his errand. He felt it was urgent. It was already the latter part of March. The weather was warming and the wagon train would soon be starting. He wanted to be ready.

He came back about an hour later with a tall stranger beside him. Sax stared at the giant, as he had never seen anyone so tall. The man was about six foot four inches tall with hair and beard a coppery flame in the afternoon sunlight. His eyes, above deeply tanned cheeks, were piercing blue. He was dressed in buckskins, as some of the men in town had been.

"Martha, this is the man who will be wagon master, Rod MacGregor. He'll be guidin' us, at least as far as Fort Laramie, where we'll be branchin' off from the main wagon train."

She straightened from the campfire, where she had coffee brewing, brushing a stray curl back, as she did so. She offered her hand to the colorful stranger.

"Pleased to know you, ma'am," he acknowledged. "Your husband has been asking about the necessary supplies for your trip, among other things. So I have made a list of things that are considered essential. You can compare them with what you have and decide what else you will need. "He handed her a piece of ruled tablet paper, covered with writing.

John spoke up, "We just might be in luck about that wagon ah told yuh we'd hafta get." he said, jerking his head toward MacGregor, "that one was built for some guy who decided not tuh go. So maybe if we hurry, might get it 'fore somebody else."

The two men strode off together in the direction of town. Martha glanced at the paper in her hand. Written in a firm, legible hand; it stated that most lists were compiled for those going to California or Oregon, but since they were going to Colorado it could be adjusted accordingly. Recommended per person were two hundred pounds of flour, one hundred fifty pounds of bacon, ten pounds of coffee, twenty pounds of sugar, and ten pounds of salt. Other commodities listed were rice, tea, beans, dried fruit, baking soda, vinegar, mustard, lard, and other optional items.

Martha sighed. She had enough of some things, thanks to her hard work the previous fall. Her flour supply, though, was much too low. So was the coffee, rice, sugar and a few other items. She hoped they didn't run out of money. They had a pretty good nest egg from the sale of everything, plus a small savings, but by the time they bought wagon and oxen or mules plus supplies and the cost of ferry crossings and other unexpected expenses…well, she wasn't as complacent about the whole thing as John was. She sighed again. First things first. She must prepare the evening meal now and worry about the rest later.

John returned well pleased. He had struck a deal with Boggs, the wagon builder. He had acquired the wagon plus four yoke of oxen to pull it. In return, he was to trade his smaller wagon, the chestnut mares and $300. He considered it a good deal. He felt a little bad about trading off Martha's mares, but insinuated they wouldn't have the stamina for the trip anyway.

He was in a jovial mood that evening and even got out his fiddle as they were enjoying the warmth of the campfire after their meal. This proved to be a good ice-breaker. Soon there were many of their fellow emigrants crowding around to introduce themselves and get acquainted.

Martha enjoyed the evening more than any since she had learned of their journey. She was especially attracted to one young woman. Only eighteen years old, Velina Hooper was going west with her husband of only a few months. She was a tiny blonde girl with great dark eyes almost too large for her small face.

Velina considered the trip a great adventure and was bubbling with enthusiasm. As she said good night to Martha, her parting words were, "Oh! We're going to have such a happy time!"

As Martha got her family settled for the night, she thought, *Velina, I do hope you're right.*

The next morning was cold and overcast, so they hurried through the morning chores so they could go exchange wagons before it stormed.

Martha was impressed with the new wagon. Sturdily built of seasoned hardwood to withstand extremes in temperature, it was a good ten feet wide and half again as long. Wooden sides extended up two feet, with a double thickness of canvas stretched over bows of bent hardwood, extending up another five or six feet. The canvas had been oiled to make it as rainproof as possible. The wagon bed was well-caulked on the bottom, with tar, so that it could be floated across streams if necessary, once the wheels were removed. A bucket of tar hung from the side for future use.

"Y'all an' the younguns can sleep in this'n," John said. "It's plenty big "nuff. Joe an' me can sleep under the tarp or wagon."

Turning, he addressed the builder. "Now, Boggs, what about some spare parts…spokes, axles, and such? Got any fer sale? An' water barrels, grease buckets an' the like. We'll be needin' them."

Concluding their business with Boggs, they set about transferring their belongings from the old onto the new wagon. Then they drove into town to pick up the additional supplies that were needed. Although they spent no more time than was necessary, Martha felt very ill at ease from all the admiring stares she was receiving, and was glad to be back at their campsite once again.

The threatened storm never materialized, so the rest of the day was spent rearranging the contents of the two wagons. Martha was happy with the additional space and was better able to organize things so she would know where to locate them. She wanted her small trunk available at all times. In it she kept a few small treasures, such as her Bible and a few photographs. Also in it were her medicines, such as Quinine, blue mass (a Quinine derivative), whiskey, rue and blacksnake root (for snake bite), and citric acid which was an antidote for scurvy. A little bit of it mixed with a few drops of essence of lemon and sugar and water made a fine substitute for lemonade. She had a variety of dried herbs and a good supply of matches, carefully stored in a stopper jar.

With the additional space, they were also able to take several large sacks of grain, which they could dole out to their livestock if it became absolutely necessary. They hoped it wouldn't, because it wouldn't last long. They were hoping for enough grazing along the way for the animals to survive on.

The next few days were spent teaching Martha the rudiments of driving four span of oxen. She had only driven a team of horses before, so had to learn the difference, which was considerable.

One day a lone vagabond wandered into camp with nothing but a backpack. He was planning on walking the whole distance, as he had not so much as a horse. They soon struck a deal with him. He would do the major part of the driving for Martha in return for his meals. They were curious about him, but in that era, not too many personal questions were asked. So they were happy with the arrangement. They were just to call him Charlie.

Sax and Charlie soon became staunch friends. The man was quiet, almost taciturn with most, but to the boy he showed another side, patiently answering questions or telling him an occasional story. He often gave him some little animal he had whittled in the evenings. He soon became a favorite of Lucy and Elsa, too.

Charlie was not an old man, probably no more than forty, but looked as if life had given him some hard knocks. His hair was almost totally white and his brown eyes had a sorrowful expression, as if they had seen too much suffering. His shoulders were prematurely bent and his body was thin. He was knowledgeable and willing to pitch in wherever needed, though, and was to be a great help to Martha on the long trip.

They had only a short while to wait until the weather moderated enough for the signal to move out. Excitement was high and it seemed that bedlam was going to prevail, but somehow, the tall figure of MacGregor was everywhere, creating order out of confusion, giving a command here or a gentle word there.

Each wagon was given a position and told to keep it throughout the journey, with the responsibility of any livestock they were taking with them. Gradually the converged wagons of the campsite became a long, serpentine stream, heading west.

Martha had spent the last evening writing letters, to be sent while she could. She wrote to Sam and to her sister, Sarah, telling them of their trip to St. Joe and their wait at that place.

"All around us," she wrote, "are more cattle and horses…and even sheep, than I ever saw in my life! On both sides of the river; and wagons galore. Some of them I got my doubts about making such a trip. They're just not sturdy enough. Ours, though, is good and strong and bigger than I ever would have believed. And the people! You just can't imagine the throngs of people who are here…all going west!"

She continued, "I've been cooking for years and years, but this is something different to me. Squatting around an open fire in all kinds of weather is not my idea of the way to cook a meal! With the Lord knows how many trips back and forth to the wagon. By the time the dishes are done and things kinda lined up for breakfast, it's past bedtime. I tell you, I've got to get myself a better way of organizing things!"

CHAPTER 5

The first day of their journey, with all the confusion being sorted out, they did not make many miles but were content. They were on their way! Those going to California and Oregon couldn't expect to arrive before October or November, and those going to the Shining Mountains would not get there before August, at the earliest.

The wagons were circled for practice. MacGregor said,"We wouldn't have to do it yet, but you may as well get in the habit. When we reach Indian country, it's a must for protection. Although the larger wagon trains usually aren't bothered. Smaller groups or stragglers are the ones in most danger."

The days gradually formed a pattern, with everyone falling into their proper places. They arose early to get breakfast out of the way, things packed back into the wagons and the animals on their way and wagons rolling. There were drovers for the livestock and at night a guard was set over the animals. All men were expected to take their turn at this.

Crossing streams was a slow, tedious process, even if there was a ferry. Goods had to be unpacked from wagons and loaded onto the ferry, taken across and reloaded into the wagons, after they had been floated across. Animals had to be forced to swim in most instances. Of course, there was a fee to be paid for any goods or people who used the ferry. If there was no ferry, they had to get across as best they could.

For Sax, it was a time of excitement, adventure and learning. Even the heavy dust of the trail, or mud, as the case was, and the constant lowing and bleating of the animals didn't put a dent in his enthusiasm. He plagued Charlie and his mother with questions, or sometimes just lay back, watching passing clouds or landscape, dreaming his own dreams.

He was pleased at the travel arrangements, as he hardly ever had to come into contact with Joe. The older boy traveled beside his father on the freight wagon, learning to handle the mules, thereby giving John an occasional break. This suited Sax just fine, since he considered his brother the bane of his existence, put there just to torment him. Not without some justification, either, as Joe always managed to give him a pinch on the sly, or a hard rap of his knuckles as he passed, or a casually thrust out foot to trip him. He was either sneaky about it or tried to cover it in the form of play. No wonder the smaller boy learned to avoid him.

Sax, however, spent happy hours with Lucy, playing quietly in the wagon or amusing Elsa. Sometimes they ran and played alongside the wagons. At other times, Martha checked their progress in the few books they had.

Evenings, Sax spent wandering around the various camp fires, listening to the stories of the men, as they sat around mending harness or spokes that may have broken on the trail. Even MacGregor became familiar with the little tow-head, and occasionally swung the boy up before him on his saddle, riding along in comfortable companionship for a few miles.

The boy listened avidly to the evening stories, some of which wouldn't have been quite so vivid, had they known Sax was drinking in every word. He heard about the mad search for gold in endless detail, of rich strikes that had been made in some instances, but also of those who had made a fortune and lost it equally as fast. He heard about Indian fights, massacres and scalping, as well as occasional stealing of white women or children. He had plenty of grist for a vivid imagination.

The early part of the trip was plagued with spring rains, which made pulling difficult for the animals, with the weight of clinging mud added to the already heavy loads. The shouts of the drivers and the crack of whips added to the din of the trail.

It was also a very difficult time for the women. Trying to keep a cook fire going was almost impossible in the wet conditions. One evening, as the fires sputtered out one by one around the area, Martha grabbed her umbrella and had Lucy hold it over the meager flame, while she fried chunks of dough which had been intended for loaves of bread. This fried bread was passed out to all the nearby wagons, which would otherwise have had nothing hot for supper. Along with some jelly, it made a filling substitute for a meal.

This occasion convinced Martha that there had to be a better way to cope than an umbrella. She asked John to tack up one edge of their canvas tarpaulin to the boards along the side of the wagon. The bottom edge could be staked down, thus making an open-ended shelter beside the wagon. She could have a small fire there, for cooking, without it getting drowned out. It could also be used as a sleep shelter for John and Joe, if they desired. When traveling, it could be rolled up and tied to the side of the wagon. This small innovation made a great difference to her peace of mind, and it was soon copied by many of the other emigrants.

Martha's relationship with Velina Hooper had blossomed into a pleasant friendship and they chatted whenever possible. The younger woman often asked her advice on minor problems or asked to exchange recipes, or just exchanged bits of gossip.

Velina's cheerful young husband, Tom, was also well-liked. His blue eyes sparkled with good humor and there was usually a song on his lips. He was often called upon to entertain around the evening campfires.

The rains gave way to constant dust and dry, treeless plains. Water had to be doled out carefully as the distances between fresh water became longer. The men's faces took on a brown, leathery appearance, and so did some of the women's, who were not careful about donning their wide brimmed bonnets. The animals also suffered through these times, their plaintive cries for water, constant.

Sax had become as brown as an Indian, his hair bleached even lighter by the hot sun. On one such hot day in late June, he scrambled down from the wagon, deciding to wait for Hooper's, who were a few wagons back. Tom had become another favorite of his, because he always had a song or story for him.

He stood beside the trail, slowly wriggling his bare toes in the dust, enjoying the powdery sensation, when he became aware of a movement near his foot. He stared, his eyes wide with terror, at the large, diamond-patterned snake, coiling and giving its warning buzz. Unable to move for fear, he stood as if his feet had rooted into the dust that he had been enjoying a moment before.

CHAPTER 6

Suddenly, he was caught up in a strong pair of arms, as Tom leaped from his wagon seat down onto the snake. However, he had misjudged the distance, and as he tossed Sax into the safety of the wagon, he felt a burning pain in his ankle. He saw that the rattler had a fang hooked in the top of his shoe and was making a bite-like movements, trying to dislodge itself, thereby pumping even more venom into him.

MacGregor came galloping up, taking in the situation at a glance. He dropped from his horse in one smooth movement, drawing his pistol with one hand and grabbing the snake with the other. He tossed it away, blowing its head off a second later.

"Hey, Jack," he called to one of the men, "stop the wagons! We got us a snake bite here!" Velina had scrambled from the wagon and hurried over as Rod MacGregor was tying a bandanna under Tom's knee for a tourniquet. "Oh, darling!" she exclaimed. "What a brave thing to do!"

"Better me than the boy." he said, through gritted teeth. "But I'm gittin' awful dizzy. Thought it'd be slower actin'."

MacGregor spoke. "It was a massive dose of venom and a huge rattler. It apparently kept injecting venom as it tried to free itself." He had slit Tom's pant leg, removed his work shoe, and cut an X-shape over the wound, which was already swelling rapidly. He let it bleed a moment, then put his mouth over the cut and tried sucking the poison out, spitting and repeating the process. "Bring some whiskey," he requested. "Maybe that will disinfect it. I wish we had a doctor along, but we don't."

Someone handed him a bottle of whiskey, which he grabbed and poured liberally over the wound. Velina was sitting with her husband's head cushioned on her lap. Her lovely eyes were luminous with unshed tears as she worriedly stroked his hair. He seemed to be losing consciousness.

MacGregor suggested that Velina get a bed prepared for Tom, while the circling of the wagons was completed. He saw that this was going to be a crisis which they would halt for. To one of the on-lookers he said, "You stay with Tom until his bed is ready and the wagons in position." He strode off to check on the latter situation.

Martha had discovered what had happened with both relief and dismay; relief because it wasn't Sax who was bitten and dismay because it was due to him that Tom was now in this grave condition.

She collected her young son and ordered him to their wagon, stopped for a few consoling words to Velina, and hurried off after Sax. She went directly to her trunk which contained her herbs and medicines, rummaging until she found a couple packets which suited her. She started a small fire and put some water on to heat.

Sax, feeling guilty and sorry about Tom, still watched his mother with curiosity. "What ya gonna do, Mama?"

"These herbs are supposed to help snakebites," she explained. "Fresh leaves of Rue would be better, crushed, but I'm goin' to soak some dried leaves in hot water and see if it's got power 'nuff to draw the poison out of Tom's ankle. If it doesn't help, I still got some powdered snakeroot to try."

Sax, looking very downcast, said, "If'n Tom dies, it'll be all my fault...oh, Mama! Ah wisht ah could do somethin'!"

"Now quit that kinda talk, young man!" Martha spoke more sharply than usual. "We ain't gonna let him die and don't you forget it!"

As soon as her dried leaves had steeped enough to soften, she took them and hurried to the Hooper wagon, where she found Tom breathing very shallowly, his leg still swelling grotesquely. Velina had been forced to move the tourniquet above the knee, as it had grown so tight it was cutting off all circulation. Martha set to work applying the herb as a compress over the bitten area. When they heated up from the poison drawn out, she discarded them and added more over the wound.

She had only a limited amount, however, and before the full benefit could be derived, she was out of the herb.

"Don't despair." she told the younger woman. "I still have some snakeroot, and we'll try it." She glanced at her friend, whose tiny form seemed somehow to have shrunk even smaller, her pale face now wet with tears.

Her heart wrenched and she put her arms around the girl." I've got to help him," she whispered, almost to herself. "If'n it wasn't for him, it'd be my Sax layin' there."

She prepared poultices of the powdered snakeroot, fastening them to the swollen limb with torn pieces of petticoat. She finally insisted that Velina try to get some rest, promising to call her if there was any change. Velina insisted she couldn't sleep, but soon the strain of events and her exhaustion won out and she was fitfully slumbering.

Martha ignored her own exhaustion and sat through the night with Tom, bathing his feverish brow and changing poultices. MacGregor came periodically to check on the man. He was touched by Martha's determination to save Tom. He noticed the dark shadows of weariness and compassion under her eyes, the little tendrils of curls which had escaped from her braided coronet of chestnut hair. He wondered, as he had many times, how John had ever won such a woman. When he spoke, however, it was only to inquire, with concern, after Tom.

It was nearly dawn when Martha finally voiced her rising fear. "I don't have any more of the right herbs to help him, "she said sorrowfully." I think the only thing that might save him now is amputation…and God forgive me, I don't think I can do that!"

MacGregor had seen men die of snakebite before, when they had no attention, although it was not common, but this was the worst case he had seen. Even with all they had tried to do for Tom, he believed she was right. He looked at the swollen limb and knew it wouldn't be long until the poison reached the vital organ, causing death.

"I believe you're right," he told Martha. "If Mrs. Hooper gives her consent to amputate, and I do it, do you think you'd be up to helping me…sewing up and such?"

Martha shuddered, as her face paled but without hesitation answered, "I'll do anything I can to help Tom live. He saved my boy."

Martha gently woke the sleeping wife. "What happened?" Velina cried anxiously, looking at her husband uncertainly.

MacGregor explained the situation to her, as her eyes widened in horror. Martha's arms tightened around her, as she told her, "We wouldn't even dream of mentionin' such a thing to you if we thought there was a chance of savin' his life any other way. Don't you see…as awful as it sounds, it's a chance for him to live! For you to still have a home and family and a good life together! He's a good man and a smart man. He can learn to do with one leg…if you don't make him feel like a cripple…if you don't make him feel less than a man!"

Velina's hands had pressed against her mouth to stifle her outcry, as she visualized her beloved Tom having to go through this mutilation, but as Martha's words sank in, she dropped her hands and stiffened her spine.

"You're right," she said. "It ain't Tom's leg I love… only as part of him…It's the man I love…that I hope to grow old with. I will never make him feel less than a man if I have anything to do with it! He is the best of all possible husbands. Please do what you can to give him back to me!"

MacGregor and Martha consulted, leaving Velina to sit with Tom. After deciding what tools were available to do the dreaded task, they set about gathering the necessary items. While the wagon master went to get more whiskey and a couple of strong men, Martha went to tell John what was happening and to gather needles, thread, healing herbs and clean cloth for bandages. She asked John to bring his saw.

They met back at the Hooper wagon a few minutes later. A table was improvised with a sturdy headboard from a bed, volunteered by someone trying to take a treasured keepsake from home. They placed it across a couple of chests. Tom was carried out and placed on the makeshift table. The saw was cleaned and doused generously with whiskey. Martha also dipped her needles and thread in whiskey. After washing their hands, they were ready to begin.

Martha asked Velina to go to her wagon and stay with the children, as they didn't want her to endure the ordeal of watching. The men, who were helping, took firm grips on Tom to keep him from thrashing around. John tried to force some whiskey down his throat and poured some on his leg where they were going to cut, above the swelling, then stepped back out of the way.

Martha sent up a silent prayer that she wouldn't faint and that God would bless their attempt to help Tom. MacGregor took the saw and soon had the grisly job done. In spite of his unconscious state, Tom tried to fight the men who held him. It was all they could do to keep him still enough. The wagon boss cauterized the stub of leg with a hot poker to eliminate bleeding. John poured whiskey down the struggling man. He finally sagged into limpness and Martha stepped forward to do her part.

She tried to push the actual facts to the back of her mind, and swallowed hard to control the bile that threatened to come up. She concentrated on taking neat, tiny stitches as if she were doing a piece of embroidery, as she sewed the flaps of skin over the end of the stump.

At last it was finished and she gave a quivery moan, as she turned to reach for some of her dried comfrey leaves, which had been soaking to soften. She made a poultice of these and put over the stitched area, binding it with a clean cloth. She saw that Tom was gently moved back to his bed, and then ran away from the wagon, retching, tears flowing down her cheeks.

John awkwardly followed and squeezed her shoulder. He was amazed that she'd had the strength to do the distasteful job, but not knowing what to say, he soon left. Trying to compose herself, Martha was startled to feel another touch on her arm. This time it was MacGregor.

"I just wanted to thank you and say how well you did. I know how difficult it was for you. But I think Tom has a chance now."

She gave a tremulous little smile, her face still damp with tears. "I pray he will live. The comfrey has real healing power and will help keep the swelling down. I hope it will be enough."

The man looked at her with admiration and sympathy. He had hated doing his part in the operation so felt he understood her feelings about it. "Get some rest," he told her gently. "You're exhausted. We will stay here an extra day to see how things go."

She stumbled to her wagon to tell Velina that for now they had done all they could. "I will be over later to change his poultice, but if you need me before then, call me."

The day of rest did everyone good and gave opportunity to catch up on neglected chores. Martha spent most of it with Velina and Tom, taking turns with the girl sponging his feverish face, moistening his dry lips with precious drops of water and making him as comfortable as possible.

She insisted that Velina rest the first part of the night, telling her she would call her for the latter half. Along toward midnight, Tom started moving restlessly. Martha saw by the flickering candlelight that his eyes were open and rational.

"Velina?" he rasped, as his tongue flicked his dry lips.

Martha said quietly, "Your wife is asleep for a bit. I'll call her in a minute." She raised his head so she could give him a few sips of water.

"You really gave us a scare."

"I remember the snake," he answered a little shakily.

"Yes, but I want to prepare you…before I call Velina." She hesitated, wondering how to go about this dreaded confession.

His wide eyes were questioning as he asked, "I guess I've been awful sick?"

"Yes, but not just…sick." She paused again, and then plunged ahead. "The thing is, you were dyin'. We all thought you couldn't make it…except…by takin' your leg off…so that's what we did'"

She couldn't bear the look of shock, and through her tears, cried out," Please forgive us! As God is my witness, it was the only way!"

Tom looked at her tired, compassionate, tear-stained face and slowly covered her hand with his large, kind fingers, pressing gently.

"Don't sorrow so, Martha. My leg for my life is a pretty fair exchange; I would say…I will learn to get by."

Martha pressed a kiss on his pale cheek and turned away to rouse Velina.

"Oh, Tom, darling! You're awake at last!" she greeted him. "I was so worried. I love you so much!"

Martha slipped out of the wagon to give them some privacy. She crept quietly to her own bed, tired but satisfied that all would be well in the Hooper household.

The following day she killed one of her prized hens and made soup, taking some of the nourishing broth to Tom. He drank it hungrily, giving proof that he was recovering. "I will leave you in your wife's able hands," she said as she was about to depart.

"Charlie will drive your wagon for a few days so you can devote yourself to Tom's care," she told Velina.

The younger woman threw her arms around Martha. "I don't know what I would have done without you!" she murmured.

CHAPTER 7

Velina was a cheerful companion for Tom and encouraged him greatly. He gained strength rapidly and retained his happy nature. He was soon singing and whistling again like before and in demand around the campfire as entertainer, as he always had been.

He also discovered that he had quite a mechanical ability, and helped repair wagons, yokes and harnesses in the evenings. As he rode in the wagon, rifle beside him, he repaired boots and shoes for anyone who had a need. In fact, he made himself even more useful than before. He made himself a crutch, but as time went on, he experimented with a peg leg, which he strapped to his stump. He worked on it and refined it until he had one that was quite comfortable to wear.

At first, he had to depend much upon Velina for various chores, but gradually became proficient at most things again. Many times it was said of him, "He shore does put to shame some of those fellers who do nothing but complain!"

Sax spent much time with Tom, offering to help in small ways whenever he could. He felt guilty at first, feeling he was responsible for Tom's condition, but the man, himself, soon helped the boy back to their original, comfortable relationship. He, then, didn't feel like he had to spend all his time with Tom…to somehow give his legs to Tom.

They had seen Indians a few times in the distance, but the wagon train was large enough to discourage attacks. They were only watched. In turn, guards were doubled to watch the stock and wagons at night.

Looking across the prairie, it deceived one into thinking it was almost flat. In reality, it was one gully or hill after another. There had been variations in topography here and there. Along some of the rivers had been tall sandstone bluffs which had caught the sinking rays of the sun in rosy hues. However, in many instances, they were not considered things of beauty so much as obstacles that had to be surmounted.

They eagerly looked for each landmark along the route. The Platte River was also sometimes called the Nebraska, from a Sioux Indian word meaning "shallow". It flowed through Nebraska and Wyoming.

Chimney Rock was a tall spire of core rock, whose soft outer covering had been stripped away through the ravages of time. It had become one of the better known landmarks, which the travelers were alert to spot.

Beyond it, some two or three travel days, for a wagon train, was Scott's Bluff. Here, broken hills drew together into ridges and low ranges, with scrubby cedar trees scattered here and there. These hills reached a height of eight hundred feet above the Platte, which flows along the base of the bluff. The trail had followed the river somewhat closely to this point. Here, however, it branched into several routes through the hills.

This North Platte valley had early been discovered as a route for fur traders and later used by trade caravans taking supplies to the mountain rendezvous points and returning furs to St. Louis.

MacGregor entertained the travelers around the camp fire the night they spent by the bluffs, giving one of several versions of how they were named.

"There was this young fellow, name of Scott," he began, "who worked for a fur company. He had been with a group to the mountains for furs. On the way back, he got mighty sick. He wasn't able to stay in his saddle. He was up the river a number of miles.

Anyway, the leader of the outfit put him in a bullhide boat and left two men with him. Told them to take him downstream and they would meet up at these bluffs, saying his group would wait here for them."

He paused to point out the general area referred to, then continued. "Well, somewhere along the line, they either capsized the boat or something like that. Anyway, they lost their gun powder and supplies, leaving them in a pretty sorry position. Then, when they did reach here…their meeting place, they discovered that their people had gone on without them."

MacGregor glanced around at his listeners, and then continued;" telling poor Scott that they were going out to try and find some food, his companions left him and set out to overtake their party. The next spring some travelers found the poor devil's skeleton, and since then the place has been called Scott's Bluff."

The wagon master added, with a smile, "Of course, that's just one version of the story. There are quite a few. Some have Scott being an old man and working for a different company or at a different job or some other difference. The one thing agreed on is that a man called Scott was left here by companions and died. At least, a skeleton was found which was assumed to be Scott."

Sax, as always, listened avidly to the story. He would have preferred a happier ending, wishing Scott's companions had come back and saved him, but young as he was, he had learned that things don't always happen the way you wish.

MacGregor rose smoothly from his seat on the ground near the camp fire, ready to take his leave. By the way," he said casually, "a couple more days will bring us to Fort Laramie. I know some of you will be leaving us there, heading to the mining camps in Colorado. Others will soon be taking a different route going to Oregon. The rest will be staying with me, on to California. Anyway, we'll be stopping at Fort Laramie an extra day or two to get sorted out."

Sax had been excited when the guide made the announcement, "Yonder is the land of the Shining Mountains! The mighty Rockies!"

He had pointed a strong brown finger toward the west. Sax had looked eagerly but was disappointed. He could see nothing but more prairies, with blue skies and hazy clouds on the horizon. He said as much to his mother.

She had smiled, lifting him to the wagon seat beside her. Taking his hand, she pointed his finger, sighting his eye down it as if it was the barrel of a rifle.

"Now, look real close, son, the mountains are a real pale blue from here, and blend right in with the sky. The snow on the top looks like clouds."

The boy looked long and hard, finally saying, "Ah think ah see 'em…but not real shore."

"Never mind," Martha said. "As we get closer, they'll be plainer."

Then she made a remark that captured his imagination. "You know, son, the eagles build their nests in the highest places. That's what we're goin' to do. We're goin' where the eagles live!"

As they neared Fort Laramie, there was a magnificent view of a mountain peak, which MacGregor told them was called Laramie Peak.

"Fort Laramie is considered sort of a symbolic gateway between plains and mountain country," he said. "Guess one reason is because there's such a good view of Laramie Peak about forty miles out. A good share of the year it's snow-capped, so makes a pretty majestic setting."

"How big a settlement is it?" someone asked.

"Well, I can't rightly tell you how many folks are around there, but sometimes it's a sizable number. It's one of the places they have an annual rendezvous. Mountain men, trappers, Indians…people for hundreds of miles gather to trade and have games and contests of skill.

Normally, of course, there's quite a number of soldiers stationed there, and there are quite a few settlers in the area now, drawn, no doubt, by a feeling of safety brought on by the fort. There are nice solid houses, not just cabins. Several fine buildings. It's altogether a nice little settlement."

As Sax saw the mountains loom taller as they came nearer, his heart beat in anticipation. He came from rolling hills but nothing like these giants! As they neared Fort Laramie, he was more engrossed in the beautiful peak, called Laramie, than the fort.

However, when they stopped, he was soon caught up in all the activity around him. The large wagon train was dividing into three separate ones, with the Saxon family in the smallest group. MacGregor was with the largest. The Hoopers were going with him. The group going to Oregon had been fortunate to find a few traders who were ready to start the trip back to Astoria. They agreed to act as guides.

The Saxon party, too, had found a man who knew the trail to Denver and was willing to act as guide. John had been to Santa Fe in his younger years but not by this route, so they all considered themselves lucky to have some experience to rely on. Jack Carter, wiry and tough, was a grizzled, tobacco-chewing fellow, who came with good recommendations at the fort.

The last night together was an emotional one for many of the immigrants. They had formed strong bonds of friendship over the long trail. Martha felt especially sad at saying farewell to the Hooper's. She had come to love Velina dearly and the trying vigil over Tom had drawn her close to him, also. She felt she owed Sax's life to him, never considering that they felt that way about her, in regard to Tom's life.

Sax, too, hated to part with Tom and MacGregor but was glad that Charlie had decided to come with them. Missing the others, he stayed especially close to the bent-shouldered man.

Martha had managed to piece together some of Charlie's background during the long weeks of travel. Much of it had been bits and pieces of information given to Sax in answer to his questions. Some had been small things he had said to her. And she admitted to herself, some of it she had guessed but felt sure she was not too far amiss.

Charlie had been in the war, had seen terrible atrocities, and had been taken prisoner. When he was finally released at the end of the fighting, he had returned home to find his beloved wife and little son had been killed when their house had been fired by the opposing army, trying to chase out nonexistent enemies they thought to be hiding there.

Charlie no longer wanted to stay there. His health was broken, his family gone and he became a bitter, disillusioned vagabond. He had been working his way westward when he had joined the Saxon's. Something about Sax reminded him of his own son. His grief-hardened heart started to thaw around the boy and his sisters. He also admired Martha greatly. He had mixed feelings about John. He considered him a fair man in his dealings with others, but he didn't think he was a very good husband. At least, he didn't have the warmth of feeling toward Martha that Charlie had felt for his own wife. In fact, during the long trip, John had hardly associated with Martha, except for meals. Charlie found this hard to understand, but of course, kept these thoughts to himself. His quiet glances, however, took in more than anyone supposed.

CHAPTER 8

As they traveled southward, to Colorado, more mighty mountains came into view. Then they were in the foothills of the giants. Sax couldn't get enough of them. He couldn't express his feelings then, in words, but his love for these mountains would never leave him. He looked for glimpses of the soaring eagles, remembering his mother's phrase and smiled happily to himself as he thought, "We're goin' where the eagles live!"

Perhaps, because they'd had no problems with Indians on the whole trip, the immigrants had grown a little careless, and so they were startled at Carter's yell of "Indians!" and to see a small band of warriors on a nearby hillside. They saw them stretch low across the necks of their ponies, giving blood-curdling cries, as they galloped toward the wagons.

Carter spat a stream of tobacco and yelled, "Circle the wagons behind those boulders up ahead. Hurry!"

The drivers raced madly for the designated cover, whipping the animals with frantic lashes. Children were ordered to lie down in the wagons, women dragged out rifles and ammunition for the men.

Hurriedly circling behind the large boulders, the men sent volleys of shots at the charging Indians, who drew back to regroup for another attack. During the brief respite, the women gathered the children into a hollow between two wagon-sized boulders, the best protected area.

Carter spat his usual stream of tobacco juice, saying in disgust, "That's ole Buzzard Wing and his renegade bucks. Even most o' the Indians hate his guts! He's a Ute, and they're usually friendly—but he's just plain mean! He took a white woman from a wagon train some years back. He made her his squaw. Needless tuh say white men hate his guts, too!"

Further conversation was quelled by the fresh onslaught of the Indians. John took special note of Buzzard Wing, however. His features were easy to remember- a long, hooked nose, close set eyes, pock-marked face and a nasty expression.

The Utes were just a small rag-tag band and it was soon obvious they had underestimated the ability of the little wagon train to defend itself. There were some crack shots among the immigrants and they were soon seeing the effect in fallen Indians. It was a short but heated battle. The Indians decided to leave, but not before Buzzard Wing made rude, obscene gestures and called out some taunt, which the travelers couldn't understand but could roughly guess, the meaning of.

When they considered it safe, they checked their casualties. None dead, but two men were wounded. Martha volunteered her services again and soon had the men bandaged and cared for. They proved to be minor flesh wounds, which would heal quickly.

Carter suggested they stay where they were for the night, since there was some protection and they found a spring of good water nearby. John questioned Carter at length about Buzzard Wing. He had a hunch that their paths would cross again and he wanted to know all he could about the renegade.

"Wal," Carter said thoughtfully, "I can't rightly tell you much about him. Like I said before, most Utes are friendly. Old Chief Ouray is well known and liked among the miners down around where he lives. But Buzzard Wing ain't welcome anywhere. He took his white squaw some twenty years ago, I reckon, after burnin' the small bunch of wagons she was with. Don't know who she was, though."

He spat a stream of his ever-present tobacco juice and wiped his mouth with the back of a gnarled hand. "He holes up somewhere in the mountains beyond Denver City. I've heard he has a half-breed daughter. She must be eighteen to nineteen years by now. And that's as much as I know about the bastard."

After the encounter with the Indians, the men were extremely watchful but saw nothing further of them. A few days later, they arrived in Gold Brook.

Sax and the girls stared in wide-eyed wonder. They had been amazed at St. Louis, and the bustle of activity there, but it had shown aspects of its many years of settlement. This place was different. It was pure bedlam, raw, rough and untamed. Everything had the appearance of still being on the move. Wagons even served as *hotels*, with men sandwiched in every available inch, sleeping in shifts.

The camp seemed to be one long serpentine community, winding through the canyon that followed the creek known as Nevada Gulch. The miners had been too busy prospecting to build decent shelters, so it was a sprawl of dugouts, tents, and wagons. Here and there, a few more permanent cabins were appearing, stair-stepping up the sides of the gulch, but they were few and far between. Some wooden structures had been erected for stores, saloons, and such, but many still did business in tents and from wagons.

The din was such that the girls covered their ears to drown out some of the sound. Shouts and curses rang out in a variety of languages, bawdy laughter, the braying of mules, whinny of horses, pounding, clanking and creaking all combined to make an unintelligible racket.

On all sides there was a conglomerate mass of humanity; well-dressed men of culture mingling with the ignorant and uncouth. Men of refinement jostling against cheap adventurers and dance hall girls, with painted faces and wearing short, flounced skirts. Gamblers entangled with mule-skinners, drunkards, and thugs. Most carried guns. They all seemed to have one thing in common- a certain gleam of madness in the eye, the lust for gold.

Martha hoped they would pass through this disquieting place quickly, but to her dismay, she saw

John give the signal to halt. He dismounted from his wagon, walking to hers with quick strides. "You wait here. Ah aim to make a few inquiries in there." He gestured toward one of the larger board saloons, his feet following his gestures.

Martha was grateful for Charlie's quiet presence beside her. She was quite unsettled by this place and its raw, untamed energy, although she tried to hide her qualms under a calm outward appearance. She learned that her fears were well-founded when John returned. "We're stayin' here in Gold Brook for now," he announced jubilantly. "Ah'm goin' to haul for one of the bigger minin' outfits!"

Finding a place to live proved no easy matter, however, as practically every square foot around the early claims had been staked out and filed on. John finally found a disillusioned prospector who had filed several small claims a couple miles from Gold Brook. He sold his interests to John for enough money to get back east and left with a sign the reverse of what had begun his adventure. He started with high hopes, like many others, and a painted "Pike's Peak or Bust!" scrawled on the canvas of his wagon. He left with one saying, "Busted, by God!"

John didn't have time to erect a proper house or cabin, since he had to start work immediately for one of the major mining companies which had come on the heels of the first major gold strikes. They would make do for awhile with the small cabin the prospector had thrown up, butted against the hill, leading into a small dugout.

John regretted that he had given Martha a choice in making the westward trek. He finally admitted to himself that he would have preferred coming alone, that he really didn't want to be tied down to a wife and family. He hated to admit that the fault was in himself. It would have been easier if he had reason to blame his wife, but she had been exemplary. He knew, too, that she had been deeply hurt by his gradual withdrawal but had hardened his heart, until it was second nature to ignore her needs. During his time away, his mind was occupied with things other than family.

Charlie set about building a crude shelter for himself nearby but separate, while Martha went to work to make the little cabin more livable and homey. John seemed to take it for granted that Charlie would be there to look after his family.

Charlie had privately come to the conclusion that John was a fool. Being in such close daily contact with Martha, he had become aware of her many fine qualities. She was not only lovely to look at, but had a sweet and patient disposition, was a good mother and a good friend, and completely loyal to John, in spite of his lack of attention. She worked hard at whatever task came to hand and was quick to lend a helping hand to anyone in distress.

Charlie sighed. "If things were only different," he thought. He admitted to himself that he had come to love this slip of a woman and her children. They had given him back a reason for living. Having the high morals which he did, he also admitted that nothing would ever come of his love, but he privately vowed that as long as he was allowed to he would be near to watch over Martha and the children.

CHAPTER 9

Sax loved to go exploring the countryside and gradually increased the distance he roamed, becoming a familiar sight to the prospectors and others in the area. At first, Martha worried when he disappeared for very long, but he seemed to have a built-in sense of direction and time, and always returned to tell her of his adventures.

When a deer came to drink from a pool he was lying beside and only flicked its ears in his direction and calmly lowered its muzzle to the clear water, apparently unconcerned, he was thrilled and eager to tell his mother. He watched the squirrels chasing each other up and down trees or gathering pine nuts to store for winter. He told of porcupines, beaver, or skunks he had seen. Or bright birds flitting through the forest, and the eagles he watched, soaring high overhead, as he lay on his back watching them.

Martha smiled as she listened to her young son. He was becoming like a wild creature himself, she thought, the way he had learned to come and go so silently and quickly.

She had much to do, though. Winter was going to come quickly this year at this high altitude. She had no garden produce to put up this year, or hogs to butcher. Everything would have to be purchased and the prices were shocking to her, they were so high. She carefully took stock of what supplies were left from their long journey and was disheartened. Their money was practically gone and although John had a job, she didn't know when he would be paid or even when he would be home.

Her milk cow had made the trip much leaner but still fairly healthy, and she had learned that somewhere on the trip, a bull had bred her and she was expecting a calf. Martha smiled at that. It was an unexpected blessing. She still had four hens and a rooster, so hoped to raise some chicks in the spring. In the meantime, the hens had been faithful about laying most of the time.

Charlie volunteered to go hunting for game for winter meat as soon as he had his shelter and a small shed for the animals built. Martha had discovered quite an abundance of wild berries not too far away, so she took the children one day and they picked a good supply. She used the last of her honey and made jam from the berries. Then one day, Sax came and told her he had found a bee tree in one of his wanderings.

Charlie went with the boy to check it out and found it was true. A large swarm of bees had their hive in the tree. He cut the tree down and started a smudge pot burning nearby to drive the bees away so he could get the honey. They collected a tub full, which was stored for winter.

Martha had made their humble quarters as cozy as she could have with the children helping as much as possible. They had chinked the walls of the cabin with clay from along the creek bank, packing it between the logs as tightly as they could. They dug up grassy sod and recovered the roof with it.

In the dug-out, she had sprinkled water on the dusty floor and packed it down until it was almost as smooth and hard as concrete. Then she had done the same to the walls, mixing mud and smearing it over them until they were fairly smooth and hard. She had pounded wooden pegs into the wall to hang clothing on. She had hung blankets to divide the log portion into two rooms, making one area for sleeping and one for cooking, eating and so forth.

There had been only one crude bunk along one wall of the cabin, so Charlie had reinforced it and made a couple of small double bunks out of saplings for the children. These were put in the dug-out. Martha had gathered arms full of fragrant fir boughs, making mattresses of the softest portions and covering them with soft blankets. The children loved sleeping on them, enjoying the aromatic smell.

One side of the cabin had a fireplace, made of rough stone. In this, she cooked in her Dutch oven and the little tin oven she baked in. The floor of the cabin was dirt, so she packed it down as she had done the other room, making it easier to keep clean. She had brought a few of her crocheted rugs. These she scattered on the floors, creating a little color in her drab surroundings.

There were two tiny windows, minus glass. Charlie saw the need of covering them for future warmth, so he made heavy shutters out of the same type of saplings he had used for the bunks. Martha was able to open them for a little light but could close and bar them for warmth and protection. She hoped someday to have glass in them, as she hated the sunlight being shut out.

A rustic table and benches, along with her trunks and a few personal items, completed her furnishings, but there was room for little more, anyway. A few shelves were put up to hold necessities and it was the best they could make of it.

No formal school had been established in the mining community, but a young lawyer, Jim Hornwell had offered to devote two days each week to help any interested youngsters to learn their basic three Rs. When Martha learned of this, she insisted her children participate, except for little Elsa. Joe quickly learned to play truant, unknown to his mother.

Joe's disposition had grown surlier as each month passed. He had come to despise his father and didn't try very hard to conceal it. He had always considered Sax a nuisance and his little sisters as silly pests. He had a grudging love for his mother but wanted desperately to be out from under her discipline, too. He was biding his time.

Grown large for his age, he seemed older than his years. He knew he could pass for sixteen, although he had not yet had his fourteenth birthday. He had been making inquiries about anyone going to California, hoping to slip away with the group but had come to realize he would probably have to wait until spring. He wished desperately that he had stowed away on MacGregor's wagon train but knowing the man, figured he would have found a way to return him to his parents. In the meantime, he found what odd jobs he could, trying to save a little money for his adventure.

Sax spent many hours watching the prospectors. Many used the heavy miner's pan, with a deep crease across the bottom, into which the heavy gold settled when sand was washed.

Others built sluice boxes. These were long wooden boxes which were usually placed in a series of three or four, into which a stream of water was diverted from the nearest creek. Along the bottom of the boxes, at short intervals, were nailed wooden crossbars, called riffle boards. These were to hold small pools of mercury, which caught and congealed with particles of loose gold as they sank to the bottom when dirt was washed down the trough. Sometimes, for lack of mercury, strips of heavy blanket were laid along the bottom of the sluice to catch the gold.

To ease the strain on their backs, some miners were using "cradles". These were pans, mounted on rockers or staves. Some had an improved version of the cradle, called a Long Tom. It was made from a hollowed out log or similar contraption, which could be rolled from side to side with a long handle.

Most of the miners didn't mind the boy watching. To many, he was a reminder of their families left elsewhere. Some were quite garrulous and the boy learned many things not in the school books.

Sax always passed on these new and exciting bits of information to Charlie, who gave the boy the time and companionship that his father never had. Charlie thought maybe one day he would try his hand at prospecting; maybe in the spring. He was a farmer at heart, though, and dreamed of getting some land and animals to start a small ranch.

Winter was upon them suddenly, as happens in mountain country. It was beautiful but much more difficult to get around. It was also colder than any the Saxon's had experienced before, since they were at a much higher altitude. In the evenings, Martha's knitting needles clicked busily, as she tried to keep up with the need for more mittens, socks and sweaters.

One day, Martha threw her old shawl around her shoulders, pulled the latchstring and stepped outside. She sniffed the air and gazed to the north. There was an icy chill in the air and the feel of some unseen force that was momentarily being held in check. She glanced toward the little cow shed. The cow was moving restlessly inside. She gave another appraising glance northward, wishing inwardly that John was here. However, her husband was gone again for at least two more weeks. She squared her shoulders and turned back to the house. Laying aside the old shawl, she put on a coat that would give her more freedom of movement, as well as more warmth.

"Lucy," she told her oldest daughter, "you keep an eye on Elsa. Sax, you get your coat on and come with me. We've got work to do. Sax, you gather all the wood and chips you can find and take inside, and then fill the water buckets."

Martha took the milk pail and went to the shed, although it was much earlier than she usually milked. The wind had started mildly but was gaining force with each passing minute. It howled wildly and whipped her skirts about her like long clutching fingers.

Picking up the little stool, she walked over to the cow, speaking to her in a soothing voice. There was something comforting about the simple task. She finished milking and glanced over where "old Red", the rooster and the hens were already roosting at the other end of the shed. She hastily searched the nests but found no eggs. She threw an extra fork full of hay in for the cow, grabbed the bucket of milk and made her way back to the cabin, which was already just a gray shape, as the snow had begun to come down in earnest.

She was happy to see that Sax had finished his chores and was inside with Lucy and Elsa. Joe was gone, as he was at one of his short-term jobs.

They settled down to wait the blizzard out, knowing it was not safe to wander out in it. People had been lost and frozen just a few feet from safety before. It was two days later, before they dared to venture out. Then it was a back-breaking job to clear paths through the piled up snow.

John was seldom home and money was scarce. Martha determined to start cooking meals for sale in the spring, so she could depend on herself for the children's livelihood. She knew Charlie would help her build a small lunch room if John wouldn't.

Charlie had gone to a blacksmith in Gold Brook and had been eagerly hired by the overworked man. Sam Oldman was a huge, bear-like man, with shaggy beard and soft blue eyes. His strength was legendary, but he was a gentle, soft spoken person, who became a staunch friend to the bent—shouldered veteran.

Sax was soon a familiar sight at the blacksmith shop, too. Where Charlie went, sooner or later, Sax went, also. As was his habit, he watched carefully as the smithy heated metal and shaped horseshoes or other needed items. His education was continuing, although much was from the school of life.

The boy's curiosity was boundless, though, so he didn't confine himself to the smithies. He wandered the town, watching it grow, as he was also doing. Occasionally he would earn a little money, running errands or doing some odd job. He always handed his earnings over to Martha with a proud smile.

During this time, he got acquainted with Soo Ling, the Chinese man who had started a laundry, commonly referred to as a washee house. Soo Ling wore a little round hat and had a long pig tail braided down his back. He spoke poor English in a singsong voice. Sax was fascinated by him and Soo Ling was kind to the boy, but everyone wasn't kind to him. He was often greeted with curses, even by his customers. Sax wondered how he could remain so good natured under all the abuse.

Soo Ling and his family turned out mountains of clean clothes for the community. It reminded Sax of the time he helped his mother make soap. "I know how to make soap," he told the man. "I helped Mama make it."

"Boy makee good soap. Bring Soo Ling. He buy," the man told him.

Sax fairly flew home with this bit of news for his mother. They were soon busy making a big batch of soap again. Charlie helped Sax take it to Soo Ling's establishment. The old man's face was wreathed in smiles when he saw the boy's soap.

"Boy work hard. Bring so soon!" he said in his sing song way.

Soo Ling paid the boy a fair price, telling him, "When gone, boy make more, yes?"

"Shore will!" Sax replied happily. "Now I gotta go tell Mama!" He was off and running.

They frequently made soap after that and always found a market for it, not only at Soo Ling's but at the stores and individuals.

CHAPTER 10

One day Martha awoke to the sound of shouting and many people running down the road past the cabin. Hurriedly dressing, she stepped out to see what had happened. She was told a good share of the town was in flames, started at Soo Ling's washee house. She looked in the direction of the community and saw smoke billowing over the intervening hill.

She immediately wondered about injuries. Charlie, coming from his cabin, stopped to talk to her for a moment, on his way to the blacksmith's. She asked him to send word back to her if she could help with anyone who may have been hurt. She felt she couldn't leave her children unless it was an emergency.

"If they need that kind of help, I'll come back and stay with the kids," he promised her. He didn't come back right away, as every able bodied man available was trying to get the fire under control. The fire spread from one place to another so rapidly that many of the town's residents fled to the protection of the various mine tunnels.

As Charlie was leaving the destruction for his cabin, he was horrified to see a bunch of rabble -rousers stirring up a fire of another sort. They were accusing Soo Ling of starting the blaze with some twisted "Chinese fire ritual". The poor man was being man-handled and they were threatening to lynch him. One obnoxious fellow pulled a knife from a scabbard worn on his belt, grabbed Soo Ling's braid, and sawed it off, and grinning at the Chinaman's panicky screeching. They neither knew nor cared what his hair meant to him. Indeed, the only way his life was saved was by forcing him to leave the community, and a riot was narrowly averted. Charlie was not even able to push his way through the angry mob to get near Soo Ling.

Later, it was learned that the fire had been caused by a faulty flue, but the original rumor was kept alive by the troublemakers who had started it. Martha was saddened by the whole episode when Charlie told her about it. "I just don't know how people can be so mean," she wondered, as she had so many times before.

Sax missed his kind old friend, Soo Ling. He was learning that life was not always pleasant and many good people suffered unjustly.

Many of the gold prospectors were leaving for other locations, as the word was out that the gold was petering out. Word of silver strikes was rampant now. Many of the gold prospectors, however, didn't recognize silver outcroppings. They didn't know how to work silver claims. One poor fellow worked for some time before learning it was impossible to pan silver.

There were some stamp mills (of the type used for crushing soft "blossom rock" in gold) erected, but they were a great expense. Also, they proved to be a total loss because they couldn't be used for silver.

Still, many silver communities sprang up across the state, with as much excitement as their golden forbears. Places named Silver Plume, Silver Cliff, and Silverton. It was said Silverton was named when an excited miner exclaimed "We may not have gold here, but we have silver by the ton!"

Rumors kept sifting back to Gold Brook and the Saxon family, about the silver strikes. They heard about the feud between the rival towns of Silverton and Ouray, which were a source of amusement to many.

Ouray's newspaper, "The Solid Muldoon" reported, "The mines here are producing like mad." Silverton's paper responded. "The mines are not as mad as the men who believe they are anything more than a flash in the pan."

Ouray's response was, "It's natural that Silverton should throw mud, for they have a plentiful supply of it, all their roads being between six and seventeen feet deep in the stuff."

Then the new camp of Ophir (named for a fabulous mining district of Biblical fame) was targeted by the Solid Muldoon, wishing it would live up to its illustrious name. Ophir didn't have a newspaper, so some of its citizens drove a herd of burros into Ouray. Across the rump of each was painted the name of a prominent Ouray citizen. When the county judge met his "namesake", he became so furious he could hardly be prevented from making a one man raid on Ophir.

The most spectacular silver era in Colorado, though, really began with an incredibly rich strike along California Gulch. This was the site of earlier gold rush days. It was not too distant from Gold Brook, and soon that town was booming again for the second time.

Uninhabited pine flats soon cropped up with cabins, tents, banks, grocery stores, brothels, saloons, boarding houses, lunch rooms, smelters, charcoal ovens and unsightly mine dumps. Where Soo Ling's laundry had been, an opera house was built, with walls four feet thick!

Martha's lunch room was a reality and was so busy she had hired help. She heard the gossip daily, of the silver strikes. Many stories were ridiculous, some sad, and others amusing.

The gullible ones believed the surrounding mountains were on a solid silver foundation. Every rock was examined carefully. Practical jokes were plentiful, such as the story of a broken grindstone being submitted to an assayer, who was reported as solemnly saying it ran 100 oz. of silver to the ton!

Profiteers made fortunes. Squatters were driven out, in many cases, as prices of lots jumped from $10 to $5000. Groceries sold at four or five times the cost in Denver. Martha had to pay dearly for her supplies, so she had to charge accordingly.

Hotels were sometimes tents and sometimes huge shed-like structures, lined with a double tier of bunks.

They were packed day and night, with men paying fifty cents each for an eight hour sleeping shift. Some fought for a place to sleep on drafty saloon floors or paid dearly to sleep by a warm stove.

It was not the environment that Martha had dreamed of raising her children, but surprisingly, most of the rough characters had a gentle word or smile for the children. Perhaps because there were so few of them there or perhaps they missed their own families.

There were some cabins strung out through the hills, though, occupied by Cornish miners and their families. They were a more sober lot, staying away from saloons and brothels. They could be heard on the way to the mines, singing their old ballads Likewise, at night, when they returned home. Their fresh- scrubbed wives could often be seen at the noon hour, taking them shiny tin buckets, filled with fragrant meat pasties, currant pies and other nourishing food. Envious glances often followed these singing Cornishmen.

CHAPTER 11

Sax had grown taller and stronger, with hair as flaxen as ever, and eyes as blue as the Colorado sky. Life was still an adventure every day for him. He had learned a lot in the few years they had been in Gold Brook, not necessarily from books.

His brother, Joe, had carried out his plan and ran away to California with a group of settlers. Sax hardly missed him but knew his mother grieved, so was sorry for that reason. His brother, Sam, left in Missouri, had written to his mother that he had married the Jackson's daughter. He was where he wanted to be.

So was Sax. He loved this rugged mountain country and delighted in the time he could wander the trails, watching the wild animals and learning the ways of nature. He helped around the blacksmith shop, ran errands and did chores for various shopkeepers, and he still spent some time with Mr. Hornwell, reading his books and getting a rudimentary education.

Charlie had found enough gold in his early claim, to interest some of the mining companies. He sold it to one of them and immediately took his profits and bought some land to start the ranch he had dreamed of owning one day. The property lay in a valley across the mountain from Gold Brook, which meant he had to leave the family that had become so dear to him.

"I feel it's the thing to do," he told Martha. Some people don't understand our relationship, especially with John away, mostly."

She understood but was saddened by his absence. She had depended on him so much. He had been the friend she could always count on. She was glad that he was finally getting what he wanted, though. At least, that is what he led her to believe.

Sax was heart broken, though, and begged Charlie not to go.

"I have to, son," he told the boy, as he hugged him a final time. "But I promise I'll come and see you some time. And when I get a cabin built and some livestock and such, why, maybe your mother will let you come and stay awhile sometime!"

With that hope to look forward to, Sax had to be content. The girls missed Charlie, too. He'd always been more of a father figure than John ever had. Lucy, a couple years older than Sax, had grown into a pretty girl, with long, brown curls and the gray eyes of her mother. She was a big help to Martha in the lunch room. Even little Elsa helped to fetch and carry. She was a charmer, with her golden curls and dark, blue eyes. The customers always had a smile for their little "angel", as they called her.

Martha had aged in these harsh years. Her figure was still trim, but there was a touch of grey in the chestnut hair, and sadness in the eyes. She maintained a cheerful attitude, but it was an effort of sheer will and strength of faith.

An occasional letter from Missouri would finally reach her. The railroad had reached some of the areas, but not Gold Brook. Still, the mail was more dependable than before. She treasured each letter and read each one until it was practically worn out.

She had been saddened, when her sister had written of the murder of Jesse James. She learned he had even been in Colorado prospecting, for a time. He had decided that he wanted to see his aging mother again, so had returned to Missouri. He assumed the name of Thomas Howard, as he had done in the past. He was shot in his own home by one of his old gang members, who he had supposed to be a friend.

Martha had always seen more good in Jesse than evil. She remembered when he had given her the matched mares for the old work horse. She blamed his fall to outlaw life on the war. It had changed so many lives.

She also grieved over Joe, and worried about him. She knew he was headstrong and had a streak of meanness in his nature, but he was still her son and she loved him. About a year after he ran away, Martha received a letter from MacGregor, to let her know that Joe had arrived in California safely.

"I didn't think Joe would write," he told her," but I wanted you to know he is safe at this time. He joined up with a wagon train I was guiding, having attached himself to a family going west. Apparently, he let them think he was an orphan and older than he is. Being large for his age, he wasn't questioned. I knew how worried you must be and wanted to give you what peace of mind I could."

Martha was so grateful for MacGregor's letter. "At least, Joe is alive!" she thought. "Maybe he will be alright and find what he is searching for."

Sax spent more time at Sam Oldman's blacksmith shop. Now, that Charlie was gone and the boy getting bigger and stronger, Sam was teaching him more about his trade, and using him for some of the chores.

Sam had a particular interest in one of the saloon girls, named Satin Lacey. Even though she was one of the women considered a common whore, Sam was quick to defend her and always treated her with the courtesy he afforded all women. He maintained that circumstances had driven her to her profession. He thought she was basically a good person, and she was known to be kind and thoughtful.

Sam took her for occasional buggy rides, and paid court to her in various little ways, never once acting as if she were anything other than a lady. He had hopes of persuading her to leave her sordid life and marry him. She, on the other hand, thought he was much too good for her. She had come to love the big, quiet man. He made her feel like a person of worth, not a piece of merchandise. She didn't want to bring him unhappiness.

Sax thought she was awfully pretty, even if she did use too much *paint* on her face. She had glossy, black ringlets piled high on her dainty head; black, sparkling eyes and wore bright satins and laces, as befitted her name. She was kind to the boy. He reminded her of the baby boy she had lost years before.

She often found occasions to have him run errands or other little chores for her, because she liked him and wanted to help him in some small way. She would press a generous coin in his palm on these occasions.

He asked her once if Satin Lacey was her real name. Laughingly, she told him, with a bit of Irish brogue, "I changed me name because I wouldn't be wantin' me dear old mum to be iver findin' out what me true line o' work is. Shure and it would be breakin' her saintly heart!"

CHAPTER 12

The winter had been cold and harsh. Many had died of pneumonia and other ailments. There had been an outbreak of smallpox in one of the mining communities, sending panic through the whole area. It finally reached Gold Brook. People were afraid. They often couldn't get anyone to help them or even bring food to them. Some people buried their dead secretly at night, so the mounting death toll wouldn't be known.

One day, Sax rushed to his mother. "Mama! Sam needs you quick!" She made arrangements to leave her lunch room as soon as she could and hurried to Sam's place. He was distraught.

"It's Satin," he told her. "I know that none of the so-called decent women have ever had anything to do with her, but I love her. She's got the *pox* and they've chased her out of town to die alone! Can't you help, Martha? I've always heard how you are so good with sick folks."

Martha paled. "This is smallpox, Sam! I don't know that much about carin' for it, and you know the chances aren't too good!"

Her heart went out to the big man, as well as the woman they were discussing.

"She's in my cabin, Martha. I couldn't just leave her out in the cold somewhere."

"Well, the only thing to do is for me to stay and care for her and keep everyone else clear away from that cabin. And that includes you, Sam! But first, I've got to arrange for my young ones to stay home with someone. I have to see to food and get my herbs and medicines. What about firewood and water?"

"There's a good supply of wood beside the back door," Sam answered," and a spring of water right up next to the hill the cabin's by."

As he realized she was actually going to undertake the care of Satin, he was overwhelmed with emotion. His voice was husky as he clasped her hand and said, "Bless you, Martha! I'll never forget this! And I'll keep an eye on the younguns and stay with 'em nights."

Sam went with Martha to gather the things she needed and explain her absence to the children. She often looked after someone who was sick, so they weren't unduly upset.

She was soon standing in front of his cabin with her stuff piled around her, as she wouldn't let Sam go any farther. She said he could call from a distance to check on them, but no one was to come any closer than twenty feet.

Entering the building, she saw Satin huddled under a pile of blankets on Sam's bed. She was very feverish and pustules of the dread disease had already covered her face and arms. She was only semi-conscious.

Martha carried her belongings in first, and then got a fire started. She had brought a good supply of rags, as she intended burning all that she used for cleaning the sores, wanting as little contact with the oozing matter as possible. She had also brought some sheets and extra clothing.

As soon as the cabin was warmed nicely, she stripped Satin and bathed her, burning the clothing that she removed. She dressed her in one of her own nightgowns and covered her warmly once again. Martha prepared an herbal tea, which she used for fever, and spooned it into Satin's mouth at intervals.

Believing that cleanliness helped in all sickness, Martha set to work to clean the cabin. She scrubbed and washed down everything possible. The blanket that had been next to Satin, she took outside and hung across some branches to air out thoroughly, after brushing snow across it, in lieu of laundering. She planned to do this each time she bathed and changed Satin, alternating the blankets each time. While she cleaned, she had a pot of nourishing soup simmering on the stove.

Satin had been only vaguely aware of anyone being there. She sometimes moaned or muttered, but most of the time just tossed and turned restlessly. Martha had struggled to get a little of the soup broth down the sick woman. Finally, she was quieter and seemed to be resting more peacefully.

Martha heard Sam's call, from his designated distance, and went to the door. "How's it going?" he wanted to know.

"She's alive and seems to be resting a bit better right now. But she really doesn't know I'm here. I'm doing what I can, but like I told you, I really don't know much to do."

"How about you?" he asked. "I guess I had no right to ask you to do this, but I'm grateful."

"I've always felt that a body had to do what one can, or how can you meet your Maker? Well, it's been a long day, and I'm about to get some rest while I can," Martha responded softly.

"I'll go then, and let you rest, replied Sam. If there's anything you need, tell me."

"Not now, Sam," she answered. "Good night."

The next days followed the same pattern. Martha burned all rags which were contaminated after cleaning the sores. She alternated the airing blankets and washed sheets, changing them each day. She carried in water and wood, cooked soup and brewed tea. She heated water and washed sheets and cleaned the floor. It was an endless round of drudgery, but she did it willingly, always praying for Satin's recovery.

One day, Satin looked at her with clear, questioning eyes. "You're fer bein' Sax's dear mum, aye?" she asked. "Why you be fer doin' this?"

"Yes, Sax is my boy," Martha replied, "and I'm here because that big galoot of a Sam has been about crazy with worry over you!"

The women became well acquainted in the small, confining cabin. Satin's admiration for Martha grew steadily. She was overwhelmed at the knowledge that Martha had left her own family while she nursed Satin, even knowing what and who she was. She had never seen such selflessness before.

Martha, on the other hand, had learned to know the sensitive woman that dwelt in the whore's heart. She learned how, years before, Satin had fallen in love with a man, who had promised her everything, but left her alone when he learned she was pregnant. The baby had been a boy, but only lived a short time. Satin had struggled to find work, but in the end had fallen into the same trap that had caught so many other women through the years. Her self-esteem had slipped away with her tears.

Martha was dismayed to see that Satin's beautiful face would always be marred from the scars of the smallpox. She knew, though, that would make no difference to Sam, who loved her. She urged the other woman to marry Sam when she was completely recovered. "He's a good man," she told her. "And he will always care for you."

"Shure and I do love Sam. He's fer bein' the kindest man in the world. It's just that he's deservin' of someone far better'n me."

Martha pressured her to consider Sam's happiness in her decision and she promised that she would.

As Satin improved daily, Martha failed. She knew she was coming down with the contagious disease. Satin saw it, too. "Shure and I've lived through it, thanks be to you're saintly heart! Now, I'll be fer takin' care o' you! I'll be doin' me best by you." The next time Sam came to check on them, it was Satin who opened the door to answer his call. He was overjoyed to see her looking so well again, but knew something was wrong.

"Martha?" he questioned huskily.

Satin nodded, tears running down her cheeks. "Shure and she's got it, Sam! I'll be fer stayin' and lookin' after the dear lady now. 'Tis the least I can do."

He nodded, mutely, thinking of Sax and the girls. As if reading his thoughts, Satin said, "Shure and she be wantin' you to tell her dear children how much she's fer lovin' them."

"I will. She is filled with more love than I ever saw anybody have before. Tell her they are well and I've made them stay home so they haven't been in contact with people. Maybe that will ease her mind."

As the days passed, it was Martha who tossed and turned in a delirious fever, while Satin bathed and comforted her. One morning she awoke, though, to silence and no movement from the bed. She hurried to check and was horrified to see that Martha was dead. She threw herself across the lifeless form, sobbing and caressing the pale, cold cheek. "Oh, Martha, me love! Shure and why did it have to be you? You shoud've stayed away from the likes o' me! Shure and how will we tell the younguns?"

CHAPTER 13

It was some time before John learned of his wife's death. By then, though, his life had already irrevocably changed. He had heard rumors that Buzzard Wing, the renegade Indian, was up to his old tricks. He was attacking small groups and individual wagons again. John had always been obsessed with him and his white squaw and daughter. He saw himself as being the one to right a wrong.

John had learned the approximate location of the Indian's hideout. He determined to rescue the white woman and her daughter, and put an end to his attacks on the freighters. He enlisted the support of several questionable characters who wanted some excitement, and they started the hunt.

One day they crept to the rim of the canyon, thought to be the one in which Buzzard Wing hid. To their satisfaction, the camp was there, with only a few tepees. The group of renegade Indians was small. They watched quietly and were soon rewarded by seeing Buzzard Wing, himself. John immediately recognized the long, hooked nose and scarred cheeks of the outcast." That's him," he muttered to the others." Now to see if the white woman and her daughter are here, too."

Their patience paid off when a large woman, with white hair, left one of the tents, followed by a tall, young woman with black braids. His binoculars proved them to be the ones John was seeking. The plan was to split up and charge the camp from different directions, taking the renegades by surprise. The women, of course, were not to be hurt.

The plan went well except for one slight miscalculation. John hadn't figured on the women not wanting to be rescued. The older woman had been with Buzzard Wing for so long, she considered him her husband. The younger one had known no other life. They fought like cornered animals.

Buzzard Wing was killed in the fray and his followers lost their incentive to fight after their leader's death, and took to their heels. John's group let them go. The object had been the women. Now that they had them, they hardly knew what to do with them.

The women stopped fighting when they saw they were alone. "I'm gonna take you back to the white folks," John explained to the old woman. Her response was a sullen "Why?"

"Because you were stolen and forced into that other life," he reasoned.

The adventure had lost much of its appeal to John's companions when the efforts of their rescue were treated so hostilely. Soon John found himself alone with his sullen hostages. He made a camp, determined to sort things out with the women before going farther.

He learned the young woman also spoke English, having learned from her mother. The mother's name was Clara, but had been given a different name while with the Indians, who called her Old Sage. The daughter was called White Bird. They were afraid of how they would be treated by the white people if they returned.

Privately, John agreed with them, wondering why he had been obsessed with this idea for so long. He had seen himself as some kind of hero and had only made another foolish mistake.

He studied the girl in the light of the campfire. Actually, she was not a girl, but a woman now." *Must be at least twenty four*, he thought. "Not too bad looking—don't take after old Buzzard Wing."

He noticed that she was observing him as closely as he was doing her. Something sparked in her eyes, and he felt a tingle of anticipation. Maybe this could work out after all. It had been quite awhile since he had had a woman.

Their fascination with each other grew and they were soon openly lovers. The old woman, Clara, was not pleased, but kept her opinions to herself, at least as far as John was concerned, but he heard her berating White Bird in low, sullen tones. John was determined to keep White Bird with him, however, even if it meant having Clara with them. He took them to a cabin which he had used more often than his own home. It was in a different mining camp some distance from Gold

Brook. He figured what Martha didn't know wouldn't hurt her. When news of the smallpox outbreak reached him, though, he began to get a twinge of conscience about his family. He decided he should check on them.

"Ah'm goin' away for a few days," he told White Bird. "Got some business to tend to over in Gold Brook."

When he reached that community, he went to the lunch room, called "Martha's Meals." There, he learned of her death. He remembered briefly his feelings for her in earlier times, but defiantly pushed such thoughts to the back of his mind. His heart had been amply hardened over the past few years." It's probably for the best," he muttered to himself." Now I can marry White Bird."

He made arrangements for Martha's assistant to buy the lunch room. Then he went to talk to Sam Oldman. Sam gave him the details of Martha's last weeks. When Sam saw the lack of emotion or concern, he felt a blind rage for the man in front of him. He clenched his fists to keep from reaching out and throttling John.

In a voice choked with fury, he didn't hold back his contempt." You miserable, low-life son of a dog! You're lower than a snake's belly! How you ever rated a woman like Martha, I'll never know! And such fine children- no thanks to you. I've heard about you takin' up with that breed, not knowin' or carin' if Martha was dead or alive. I oughta break you in two!"

John just looked at him with cold eyes and said, "Go to hell!" He turned around and stomped off to find his children.

"I'm gonna get married again," he told them.

At which they screamed at him. "How can you? We'll run away like Joe before we let that Indian take the place of our dear mama! We hate you!"

John was surprised that they had heard of White Bird, but didn't change his mind about marrying her. "We'll see about that!" he told them and left in a huff.

When he returned, he was in a black, angry mood, but his jaw was set in determination. "Get your clothes together!" he told them." And hurry up about it!"

He dropped Sax off at Sam's blacksmith shop, where the big man put an arm around the boy protectively.

"You'll stay with Sam for the time bein'," John said to the boy." I'm puttin' the girls in a Catholic school in Denver—they don't take boys."

"I hate you!" Sax shouted after his father as he watched his sisters being taken away, crying in each others arms.

The boy felt like he was being ripped apart. His mother was dead and now his sisters were being taken away, and his father acting like a harsh, forbidding stranger. He was ten years old and his world had just collapsed around him.

CHAPTER 14

S ax remained with Sam and Satin for the better
part of a year. He liked them and enjoyed helping
Sam around his shop. He learned a good deal about
the work of a smithy and filed it away, unconsciously
adding to his store of knowledge.

When Charlie learned of Martha's death, several
months had passed. He was devastated, for he had truly
loved her and had loved Sax as if he was his own. He
returned to Gold Brook as soon as he could, to see if
he could take the children. He knew that John had
really taken no interest in them, and he couldn't help
worrying about their welfare.

Sax was overjoyed to see him, throwing his arms
around him. "Oh, Charlie," he said softly, "I didn't
think I'd ever see you again! Ever'body I ever care about
leaves one way or 'nuther. I keep wonderin' 'bout Sam
and Satin!"

Charlie wrapped his arms around the boy, realizing
how much he had been grieving for his mother and

lost sisters, even while trying to be manly and not show it. Charlie had been shocked when Sam had told him about John hauling off the girls to Denver and his marrying the half-breed girl. It was Sam's belief that he would have taken Sax, too, but with his rebellious nature against his father, he probably would have immediately run away. After leaving him with Sam, he had never tried to contact him again.

"Son," Charlie said gruffly, for he had a hard time choking back his own emotions," do you want to go home with me? That's what I came to find out, as soon as I heard about your mother."

Sax nodded against Charlie's chest, wiping away a few tears in the process. "Oh, yes," he breathed," I'd like that a lot!"

So they told Sam and Satin, who were disappointed because they really cared for the boy. They knew, however, the close bond that had always existed between Charlie and Sax. They felt it would be good for both the boy and the man. It would probably be what Martha would have wanted. Besides, they had a happy event of their own to look forward to. Satin had learned that she was going to have a baby of her own. They knew they would not be as lonely, as they would have another young one to fill the emptiness.

Charlie kept Sax entertained on their long ride back to his ranch, by telling him tales of the more outrageous and interesting parts of the growth of the infamous city of Leadville. Some of the stories he had heard, but many were new to him, so he listened eagerly.

"They call their town the magic city. And, in some ways, I guess it is almost magical," Charlie began." At any rate, some of the strikes around there sure seemed like it! Like the world's largest silver nugget…ninety three percent pure silver and weighing more than a ton!"

Sax's eyes were wide at the thought of a nugget that big. Charlie grinned, as he continued. "Somethin' about all those riches, though, kinda makes people crazy. Well, you saw some of it at Gold Brook. But the more money some folks get, the stranger they act. Take, for instance, one fellow who was just a poor guy who couldn't even tell time. He made a big strike and the first thing he did was to buy a big diamond-studded, gold watch. He would hold it out to anyone he happened to meet and tell them, "See fer yerself the time, then you'll know I'm not lyin' to ye!" They laughed over that story, and then Charlie continued." The richer guys, they call themselves the Carbonate Kings. They want to be the leaders in everything and don't want to be outdone by any one. They think bigger and costlier is better. Some of 'em hire a bunch of personal guards —almost like private armies- and dress them in fancy uniforms, each one trying for fancier than the other guy.

When gold watches were considered the best, they have to have diamond ones; some wearing two or three at a time! Their homes are filled with the finest stuff money can buy, brought from all over the world."

They speculated on what these fine things might be like for awhile, and then Charlie continued repeating the stories he had heard and read.

"Horace Tabor is the best known of these so-called kings. He came out from Vermont where he was a stonecutter and brought his family with him. At first they went from camp to camp but never had much luck. They gave up trying to strike it rich and took up storekeeping."

"Well, how'd he get to be one of the kings then?" Sax asked curiously. Charlie chuckled." Plain dumb luck! He had taken to grubstaking a prospector once in awhile, always for a share of any strike they might make. He staked a couple German fellows and danged if they didn't just happen onto a rich vein of ore. Of course, Horace wound up with a third and in a very short time had over $500,000.

'His luck just kept running. He bought a mine which the owner thought was worthless, and in fact, had salted it with a little good ore, to make the sale to Tabor. To save face, he ordered his men to continue digging. And wouldn't you guess—they hadn't gone eight feet when they uncovered a vein of silver worth millions!"

"Wow!" exclaimed Sax.

"Yeah, but that wasn't the end of it," Charlie went on." The whole town mocked him when he spent thousands and thousands and thousands of dollars on an un-worked mine. But the laugh was on them. Tabor's mine brought in millions again. He bought interests in quite a few of the other better mines in the area and even invested in some in Mexico and South America. Oh, yeah, he got to be a real big "king". They made him the first mayor of Leadville and then he went on to bigger politics.

His private army was dressed the fanciest of them all- one group like Scottish Highlanders. In Fact, they called them the Tabor Highlanders. They dressed in kilts and the tops black and blue, trimmed with red braid. They wore fancy Bonnie Charlie bonnets like somethin' from the old country. Tabor liked to dress up in uniform, too, like a commander-in-chief.

"Course he don't live in Leadville anymore. He moved to Denver where he could be in more high society. He lives it up in style, and caused quite a scandal when he divorced his wife, who didn't like that life. Went to Washington and met a young society gal there and married her. Then it came out that he married her before his divorce was legal. Well that caused him some enemies among friends of his first wife. But with all his money, he just didn't care about the gossip."

Sax thought about this for awhile before saying," If that's what it's like to be their old king, I sure never want to be one."

Charlie put his arm around the boy, saying," well, son, there are good rich men and bad ones, the same as there are good poor men and bad ones. The thing is to be one of the good ones, no matter what size your pocketbook is."

CHAPTER 15

The next few years passed quickly and happily for Sax. He and Charlie worked diligently at making the ranch self-sufficient. The size of the herd of cattle had increased considerably. New sheds, barn and other outbuildings had been built. Men had been hired to help and had stayed on as loyal employees.

A couple of married men were among the crew, so cabins had been built for each of them. The women became the gardeners for the ranch, raising vegetables for themselves and the ranch.

A shop had been set up for the blacksmith work which is always necessary on any ranch. The knowledge learned from Sam was put to good use here, as Charlie and Sax put on horseshoes and other repairs.

Many necessities were provided by the work of their hands, but certain staples still had to be purchased from the merchants in one of the nearest towns. Charlie delegated Sax to take care of these errands more and more frequently, preferring to stay at home, as his health was declining. These trips were usually several days because of distance.

On one of these trips to town, Sax was striding down the street, concentrating on his next errand, when he thought he saw a familiar figure ahead in the crowd. He quickened his pace and soon verified his observation. "Soo Ling!" he called happily to the slight figure." It is you...I'd recognize you anywhere!"

The old Chinese man turned, with narrowed eyes, ready to slip away quickly, if necessary. He studied the sturdy, strapping young man before him, trying to place him.

Sax grinned at him, obviously happy to see him. "Don't you remember me, Soo Ling? I sure remember you! You used to buy my soap."

Recognition suddenly came as Soo Ling looked into the unforgettable blue eyes. "Yes, yes!" he chirped excitedly, almost jumping up and down in his joy." It is Sax-boy!"

They stepped aside from the milling crowd, so they could catch up on the events of the past years. Sax told him how sorry he was about the way Soo Ling had been treated and accused so falsely and run out of town. He learned that the old man had been treated badly in many places, and even now, was trying to find a place to work where he could be accepted and earn an honest wage for his family.

"Then it's lucky for me that I ran into you," Sax told him. He had told him about his mother's death and how he was living with Charlie on a ranch now.

"We could use a cook, among other things, Charlie is spread too thin, doin' too many jobs and should slow down some. You'd really be doin' us a favor if you'd come and join us," he urged.

Soo Ling was studying the young man to see if this was a serious proposition or just the kindness he'd always seen in Sax. Did he have the authority to make such an offer, the old man wondered. Remembering the close relationship between Sax and Charlie, though, he decided to take a chance. After all, it would solve his problems if it worked out. If it didn't, he would be no worse off than he already was.

"Soo Ling's family?" he questioned.

"Bring 'em along," Sax said eagerly. "We'll build you a cabin like we did the Smith's and Turner's. It'll work out, you'll see!" He impulsively threw his arms around the older man. "I'm sure glad to see you, Soo Ling."

The old man couldn't express his feelings in English very well, but he grinned widely as he felt a comfort he hadn't known in a long time. While Sax finished his errands, Soo Ling gathered his meager belongings and his two sons. His wife had died a couple years before. They piled into the wagon, along with the provisions that Sax had purchased and returned with him to the ranch.

Charlie was surprised to see the Chinese family but approved of Sax's decision to bring them home. Soo Ling, Jimmie Lee, and Chan were soon almost indispensable. They were all hard workers. Soo Ling proved to be a good cook and took over the cooking for the bunk house crew, as well as for Charlie and

Sax. And he soon had a washee house going, doing the laundry for the ranch.

Chan and Jimmie Lee were eager to learn the cowboy trade and proved to be adept at riding, roping and any job that needed doing. They were all very satisfied at the way things had turned out.

CHAPTER 16

T hings were going well on the ranch and Sax thought of his sisters. He hadn't seen them since the time of his mother's death. He had received a few letters from them through the years. They had not been too unhappy at the school. The nuns had been kind to them.

Lucy had stayed there until she had been sixteen. That was as long as she could remain. Elsa had only been eleven then and Lucy had not been considered old enough to care for her. So she had obtained work at a restaurant in Denver, where she could occasionally visit her sister. When Elsa was fifteen, she was allowed to join her sister.

The last time Sax had heard from them, they had been in Aspen, which had become somewhat of a resort town. The Hotel Jerome had been built to cater to the wealthy visitors. It had three stories, with an elevator to ride, instead of having to climb stairs. The girls were both working at this grand hotel; Lucy in the restaurant and Elsa in the laundry. They wrote that the town also had a fancy opera house which featured great singers and actors.

Sax decided it was time to visit his sisters." Who knows," he thought, "at their age now, they might be gittin' married before long—and then, no tellin' when I'd ever see 'em. Maybe I can get 'em to come back to the ranch with me."

He told Charlie of his plan and he was quick to agree that it would be a good idea. Sax saddled his favorite horse, tied on a bedroll, and put necessities and a clean shirt in the bags he tossed across his mount. He made sure he had extra ammunition for the rifle, sheathed in its scabbard, and waved good-bye.

He enjoyed the trip, as his love for this vast country hadn't abated through the years. He often remembered his mother telling him that they would live where the eagles dwell. He had felt a certain kinship with the eagles ever since and as he watched them soar; they always brought memories of Martha. He came to a halt with an involuntary gasp of pleasure, as he came over the summit of a hill, the flaming rays of a dying sun spreading like a silent scream across the dimming sky. He felt a deep sense of awe, much as he imagined the first viewers of this land had felt. Finding a sheltered spot, he made camp for the night, enjoying the serenity of the place.

The next day brought him to Aspen. He found a good vantage point and sat for a few moments just looking the town over. The Jerome Hotel was as impressive as Lucy's letter had made it seem. Indeed, it was quite a bustling community.

Then his eagerness to see Lucy and Elsa blotted out thoughts of the town. He urged his horse into a run and galloped up to the hotel. Going in, he inquired where he might find his sisters. His directions led him to the restaurant first, where he was pointed to a pretty girl with chestnut hair, pulled demurely up into a cascade of curls atop her head.

Can this be Lucy? he thought. *A grown woman!* He glanced down at his own strong, tall body and laughed out loud.

"Yes," he mused, as the girl moved toward him. "She looks like Mama."

"Hello, Lucy," he said, smiling at her." It's been a long time! I'm Sax."

She looked up at the tall young man before her, hardly daring to believe it was her brother. The pale blond hair and sky blue eyes convinced her that it was indeed her little Sax, now grown up. Tears welled up and she choked back a sob, as she hugged him tight.

"Oh, Sax, it's so good to see you again! I didn't know if I ever would. I've thought of that terrible day when we were parted so many times. It was awful! Anyway," she went on apologetically," I can't visit now; they frown on that sort of thing during work hours. But when I get off, we will have a nice visit."

She gave him directions to the little cabin, which she shared with Elsa. As he turned to go, she kissed him quickly and gave him another tight hug.

Before looking up the cabin, though, he stopped by the laundry part of the hotel, to see his younger sister.

It was another emotional reunion with both marveling at the changes the years had wrought. Elsa was still as blond and angelic looking as he had once thought her. While she couldn't get over what a handsome young man her brother had grown into. They parted with a promise of a long visit after work.

Sax stayed several days, while the siblings caught up on the events of their lives. When Sax suggested they come home with him, however, they refused. Then they filled him in on their plans.

"I'm going to be married soon," Lucy explained. "His name is Sam Miner. And he's from Texas. Right after the wedding, we're going to Texas. I'm so glad you came, Sax, before I left. It has meant so much to me."

"Me, too," he agreed." Just to know you are okay. I just wish I'd come sooner so we could have had more time together. It just seemed like there was always somethin' to be done."

"Under other circumstances it would have been wonderful to go back with you," Elsa chimed in." But I have a beau, too, and am going to marry him in the fall and go back to Denver to live. That's where he is. His name's Fred Garvin and he is such fun! He makes me laugh and sometimes that means a lot!"

"Have you a girl friend that you favor, Sax?" they both wanted to know.

"No," he answered seriously." I just haven't thought along those lines yet. The ranch keeps me busy. And Charlie is gettin' frailer all the time. Sometimes I worry about him."

"Dear Charlie!" Lucy exclaimed. "He was like a father to us, wasn't he, Sax?"

"He still is, to me," Sax replied. "He was always there for all of us, and came back and took me to the ranch with him as soon as he heard Mama had died. He is the best Dad a guy could have!" Both girls reminded their brother to be sure and tell Charlie how much they loved him.

Their talk went to a lighter vein. The girls entertained him with stories of Denver and some lively characters they had heard stories about.

"That reminds me of a story I wanted to tell you about Creede," Sax told them, with a chuckle." Seems that town got "culture…It had to have its Ladies Social Club and its book study club and its tea club and its Bicycle club!"

"What's a bicycle club?" the girls wanted to know.

"Well," Sax drawled, "this one was for women and they kinda had a uniform, of sorts. They all wore a type of bloomers—they called 'em Turkish pantaloons- in real bright colors. "Course, I suppose they was more practical for ridin' bicycles than dresses would be- but what a sight they musta been! All them ladies decked out in their pantaloons, pedalin' all over them mountain trails!"

They all laughed, imagining it. "Any way," Sax continued, "this one lady was pedalin' down the street one day, when her husband saw her. He turned as red as an old turkey's wattle. 'No wife of mine's goin' to dress so disgraceful!' he bellows." You can just pedal back to Illinois where you came from!"

"Well, by golly if she didn't take him up on it—only she went by train!"

The visit ended with laughter and tears and promises to keep in touch. Sax felt, though, that it had put a closure on his childhood. He knew he wouldn't see his sisters again for a long time.

CHAPTER 17

In the following months, Charlie's strength had improved considerably, so Sax thought it was a good time to satisfy his curiosity about the towns of Leadville and Georgetown. For years he had heard interesting stories about both. With Charlie's blessing, he planned to go check them out, with no set time to return.

"I'll miss you, son," the older man told him, "but I have plenty of good help here, and while you're young, is a good time to explore a bit."

Sax took a few extra supplies, ammunition for his rifle, and a tarp for protection from weather, and packed them on an extra horse and headed out on his adventure, waving good-bye to Charlie.

He enjoyed his time, riding through the mountains that he loved so much. He stopped to camp whenever he felt the time and place were right.

Nearing Georgetown, he was passing a small ranch, when he saw a small overall-clad figure struggling with a heavy fence post. Sax could see that the fence was down and tangled barb wire lay strewn across the ground. He reined his horse in, asking if he could help. Thinking it was a boy, he was surprised when the startled face turned to him, proved to be a young woman.

"I didn't mean to scare you," he smiled. "It just looked like you was havin' a hard time there. My name's Sax Saxon, and I was just passin' by. But my offer still stands. I'd be glad to help you with that fence."

She took in his strong, muscular appearance and pleasant smile. She couldn't help noticing that he was a fine looking young man, with blue eyes and flaxen hair. She was a bit embarrassed at her own appearance, but told herself the overalls were much more practical to work in than long skirts. So she tossed back her head and told him, "I'd be mighty glad for a helpin' hand. You see, my Pop has had a rough go of it lately. First, my Mama died. Then he had a bad accident and is laid up with a broken leg and ribs. I'm the only help he has, you see."

Sax offered his sympathy and immediately swung down from his horse and tethered both of his animals to a fence pole. Pitching in, he took the post she was struggling with, asking, "What happened here to the fence, anyway?"

"Well, this is where my Pop was hurt. Our old bull got hooked up in the wire and tore down the fence trying to get loose. Pop was getting him unhooked. And then the old devil turned on Pop. He tromped on him good before he decided to take off, leaving Pop hurt bad with broken bones."

Sax sympathized and then looked the situation over. "These posts should be anchored in the ground, not just strung on top. Makes a sturdier fence," he suggested. "I'll help you do that if you'll get the tools to dig with."

"By the way, what's your name, ma'am?" he asked, as he took in her flushed face. "You know mine."

He thought to himself, "She's mighty cute when she's all flustered like this! I like her brown eyes...they remind me of a young fawn's; and those few freckles across her nose add something special. I like her dark curls, too."

He was so busy telling himself what he liked about her that he almost missed her answer to his question.

"I'm Betsy Jackson." She smiled. "And my Pop is Dick Jackson. I do thank you for your offer to help. I can sure use it. The tools are in the barn, so if you want to put your horses there, we can grab the things you need at the same time."

After the horses were cared for and the necessary things gathered to work with, they returned to the fencing. Betsy proved to be a good helper; she just didn't have the strength for the heavier tasks. They worked steadily until the downed section of fence had been replaced. He suggested that the rest of it should be made equally strong.

"I could hang around and help do that if it'd be alright with your Pop," he told her.

"Let's go see him," Betsy answered." I want you to meet him anyway. He will want to thank you for your help. And I will fix some supper for us."

"That's a right welcome offer." He grinned. "I've ridden quite a ways and I'm not too fond of my own cookin'!"

When she had introduced her father, she left them to visit while she prepared a meal. Dick Jackson was a weathered man with tanned face and hair turning gray. His eyes were kind, but had an air of sadness about them, no doubt from the heart ache of losing his wife, and the fact that he couldn't help his daughter with the work.

"We are so thankful for your help today," he told Sax. "It's too much for Betsy, hard as she tries."

Sax's soft heart was touched. Besides, he would like to get to know Betsy better. This rather surprised him, as he had never been particularly attracted to any young woman before.

"I was telling Betsy that I could stay and help her get caught up on things around here if it was alright with you," he remarked.

Dick told him. "This is just a small, poor spread, as you can see. I can't afford to hire help."

Sax responded, "You don't have to pay me anything except room and board. That's all I need."

Dick and his daughter were both overwhelmed at Sax's offer, but were thrilled to accept it, nonetheless.

They visited and became better acquainted during the meal. Then Sax helped Betsy with the evening chores.

"I'm sorry we don't have extra room in the house," she apologized. "I'll fix you up a cot in the shed that's built on the side of the barn."

She proceeded to get it cleared and a bed made on an old cot in there and brought a lantern to hang from a rafter. Sax assured her that it would be just fine. The following day, Sax helped Betsy again, with further fencing and evening chores. They soon found themselves so comfortable with each other that they were teasing and sharing stories of their lives.

"I reckon I'll fix that barn door next if I can find another hinge for it. It's sagging pretty bad," he told the girl.

"I think there's some hardware in the barn somewhere. I'll find it for you," she responded.

During the ensuing days, as he found time he repaired the sagging barn door, replacing a broken hinge. He replaced some shingles that had blown off the house. He helped round up the few cattle that had strayed when the fence was down. Each day seemed to bring something else that needed attention. Betsy was a willing helper wherever she could assist.

In the evenings, she and her father entertained Sax with stories they had heard about Georgetown. He especially enjoyed hearing about *French Louis*, as Louis du Puy was called.

"He came from a wealthy family in France," they told him. "They say he had been a soldier and a journalist before he wound up in Georgetown. Anyway, a few years later he was hurt in a mine accident. With some money that friends collected to help him out, he bought the Delmonico Bakery. He turned it into a restaurant that he named the Hotel de Paris."

After thinking about this for a bit, Sax asked, "Go on. What happened then?"

Gathering his thoughts, Dick continued, "He dug out wine cellars underneath and added a second story with a balcony and put one of them fancy rails with metal scrolls on them. Inside, he decked it out in French finery with mirrors and paintings and fancy furniture.

"Well, sir," he continued, "He started acting like he was some king or something, and he refused to pay taxes and threatened to shoot anyone who tried collecting them! Any of his guests that didn't like the way he ran the place, he just told them to leave. He flat-out told some of the so-called Bonanza kings that they weren't welcome!

"The funny thing was; this caused his business to increase! People wanted the social status of being accepted as "gentlemen" by French Louis. It didn't matter to him if the women were "ladies" or not. He didn't care if a couple was married or not. He wanted his food and wine to be appreciated and he wanted interesting conversation."

They thought about these things, laughing among themselves, for a bit before Dick continued.

"Louis got the reputation of an innkeeper who hated his guests, and a despiser of women. To put it bluntly, he became the most talked about person in Georgetown!"

Sax told him how much he enjoyed hearing the story. "It only makes me want to look the town over more than ever," he grinned. "But much as I've enjoyed my time here with both of you, it's time for me to be moving on."

The days had turned into weeks and Dick's ribs had healed and he had been hobbling around on a make-shift crutch. He often heard their laughter and saw their smiles for each other.

"I sure hope my little girl aint' gonna wind up with a broken heart when Sax leaves," he said to himself.

He, too, liked Sax, though, and knew he would miss him when he was gone. He was surprised at how much Sax had accomplished, and kept telling him how much they appreciated his help.

"You know you're more than welcome," the young man told him. "I've enjoyed gettin' to know you and Betsy. She's a fine young woman, as you well know," he said, grinning, "But I will be heading out in a couple of days to continue my trip to Leadville. If you don't mind, though, I would like to stop back by when I head home…just to see how you're doing, you know."

He was speaking to Dick, but unconsciously, his eyes lingered on Betsy. "You'll be welcome any time at all," Dick assured him. "We're gonna miss you, young feller!"

Sax didn't admit how much he was going to miss a certain dark-eyed girl that occupied his thoughts more than any ever had before.

He wasn't much of a letter-writer, but thought he better send one to Charlie so he wouldn't be concerned about his long absence. He wrote a short note and sent it from Georgetown when he stopped to look the town over.

He wrote,

Charlie,

I've been staying at Dick Jackson's place out of Georgetown. He was laid up from an accident and only had his daughter for help, so I helped them out until he was back on his feet. I'm on my way to Leadville. Don't know how long I'll be there before I head back. Don't worry,

Sax

CHAPTER 18

He spent much of his time, as he rode, thinking about some of the tales he had heard about Leadville through the years. He knew it was situated at a very high elevation…over 10,000 feet. He had also heard how it had grown rapidly, within a year's time, from 1500 to over 18,000 people.

He had heard one old prospector tell about seeing small children, sitting in the gutters in the mornings, sifting through the sawdust sweepings from the saloons, looking for gold dust or coins that might have been overlooked. He thought to himself, "I might have been one of them kids if I'd been there."

Vivian House was owned by Charles Vivian, who had been born in England. He became an actor and ballad singer and founded a group called the Jolly Corks. They patterned their group after one in England, called the *Buffaloes*. When they decided on a permanent name for the group, they had been impressed with a magnificent elk head mounted on a wall. Looking up the history of the animal, they found it was timid, fleet of foot and avoided combat except in defense. They adopted the name and the Benevolent Protective Order of Elks was started, and eventually spread across the country.

Sax had heard that Leadville, after the introduction of electric lights to the community, was one of the best lighted cities, for its size, in the nation. Since he had never experienced lighting of this nature, he was curious about it.

The thing that had captured Sax's imagination the most was Leadville's Ice Palace. He knew he would not be able to see it, as it was gone, but he had heard there were pictures to be had, and he intended to get some, if possible.

As Sax rode into Leadville, he was disappointed. To him, it was not nearly as attractive as the area he had been living with Charlie. He wasn't really interested in the mining, except as a matter of learning. He had already watched a good many miners at work.

He had noticed that it was getting much cooler and knew that cold weather was near. He decided to invest in a hotel room for the night and check out the town the following day. He approached the clerk and asked, "Could you tell me where I might get pictures and stories about the Ice Palace?"

"Sure," he responded.

"The newspaper office would be a good place. Also, little booklets have been made about it and can be bought, as well as postcard pictures of it."

"Thanks a lot," Sax told him. "I plan on checking it out in the morning."

He learned that ice palaces were not a new idea. There had been one built in Montreal, Canada for a five day winter carnival in 1883. It was not nearly as elaborate as Leadville's, but set a pattern. One had been talked about in Leadville for a number of years before it came to pass, but conditions were not right until 1895. Much planning and concern went into the project before it could be started, but eventually work began.

Ice blocks, 20"x 30" were cut, with other sizes being made, according to their location. The total length of the structure was 450 feet and the width was 320 feet. It covered over three acres. It had octagonal towers on the north side entrance, which were ninety feet tall. The south towers and corner towers were round and were sixty and forty five feet high. Each tower had a flag on a flag staff 120 feet tall. The walls were approximately five feet thick.

Sax was amazed at the size of the structure, and even more so as he looked at a picture in the old paper. "I sure wish I could have seen it!" he thought to himself. He studied the picture for awhile, and then went back to reading the articles about it.

A warm Chinook wind in December almost ruined the structure, making extra work to get it back into shape, but by New Year's Eve, temperature had dropped down to eight below zero. Workmen beat all records by having the palace ready for the grand opening of the winter carnival on January first.

Various rooms were filled with all kinds of ice sculptures. The center section was a large ice skating rink. Ice skating, being a popular sport, attracted over 1,000 skaters the first day!

On either side of the skating rink was a large ballroom. The ball rooms were complete buildings inside the Palace. The floors were finished with Texas pine and the Grand Ballroom was decorated in terra cotta and blue.

It was a grand occasion, with parades, musicians, a group on snowshoes, and toboggans, (all ladies, dressed in red hot colors).Then, dignitaries of various sorts, miner's union, patriotic groups, fire department and groups of children. Last of all, came the workmen who had constructed the Ice Palace.

To encourage visitors from other towns, certain days were set aside and designated as Leadville Day or Central City Day, etc. During the first month, music was furnished by the Fort Dodge Cowboy Band. Local musicians were hired for the remainder of the Palace's reign. They musicians were situated on a balcony above the skating rink and Grand ballroom to furnish music for both.

Besides the Palace itself, the town had provided a variety of other entertainments for the visitors. The Ice Palace gave the town three months of carnival atmosphere before the weather warmed and the ice began to melt. By this time the town's people were rather sick of the continuous parades, costumes and excitement.

Sax grinned as he finished reading." As interesting as it was, I sure couldn't have stood it for three months! One day would have satisfied me. Still, I'm glad I came and learned about it."

He thanked the people at the newspaper for letting him go through their old files and stepped outside. He noticed at once how much colder it was from the time he entered. "I better be heading back before I get snowed in, I reckon. Maybe tomorrow I'll get a few more supplied and head out. Besides, I kinda want to see Betsy again before I head back to Charlie's. Of course I want to check on Dick, too," he reassured himself that he wasn't just thinking of Betsy. Nevertheless, as he dropped off to sleep that night, it was a brown-eyed, dark haired girl that filled his dreams.

CHAPTER 19

The next morning Sax went to a mercantile store to replenish his supplies for his return journey. While there, he was approached by another customer. "I see you seem to be a traveler like myself, "he said to Sax.

"I am Bob Wilson and was wondering which way you are heading? I wouldn't mind some company if we're going the same direction."

He had an engaging grin, Sax decided, so decided to find a little more about him before giving an answer. He introduced himself and then asked the stranger some questions, as he sized him up. The man was tall and rather thin, but looked tanned and fit. His gray eyes were direct and friendly; his hair was curly and brown and he had a small mustache above wide, smiling lips.

"Well, sir, it's true I am on a journey…actually, a return trip. Where were you heading? I know the weather is turning colder and we might run into a blizzard crossing any of the passes around here. It might be a good thing to have someone along, in that case."

"I'm going to Georgetown," Wilson responded, "and I was thinking the same about having company during a storm. My Dad is there and it's been quite awhile since I saw him. He's not gettin' any younger, you know. I figured I better check on him."

"It so happens that I'm going to make a stop near Georgetown to see some friends, so this will probably be a good thing for both of us to join forces," Sax told him, extending his hand to shake on the agreement.

They collected their gear and horses and started out. The first day wasn't too bad, just windy and cold. In the night, though, it started snowing heavily. As they were nearing a dangerously steep descent, they could barely distinguish the shape of someone else ahead of them on the trail. The wind was still blowing at a gale force. Suddenly, to their horror, the person on the trail ahead of them was enveloped in a snow-slide off the ledge above him.

'Come on! We gotta try and save him," Sax cried, as he urged his mount forward. Bob followed close behind and they were soon at the spot of the slide. They leapt from their horses and started digging through the icy snow as best they could. Soon, Sax spotted a hand sticking up near the rock ledge.

"Over here!" he yelled. Between them, it was not long until they pulled the man out. He was unconscious, but breathing. He apparently had hovered as close to the ledge as he could, which saved him from being carried down the mountain side. There was no sign of his horse, which had no doubt perished.

Their first concern was rousing the victim of the snow-slide. They learned he was also trying to make it to Georgetown. It took them much effort to clear enough snow from the trail to use it. Their only tool was a skillet that Sax had on his pack horse.

When they finally had a trail, they rearranged Bob's and Sax's gear to one pack horse so the stranger could ride the other one. They were all so cold, that their next concern was to find a place they could shelter enough for a small fire to help them thaw out. Unfortunately, it took some time to get down the steep descent. It was sheer luck that they stumbled upon an old deserted mine shaft. It went back far enough that they were able to get themselves and the horses into it, out of the wind and snow.

With the light of a match, they found some old broken timbers in the dust of the floor. So they soon had a fire going, which they sat near, huddled under Sax's tarp. When they had reached a degree of comfort, he dug out his coffee pot from his pack and made some welcome liquid warmth.

They were fairly comfortable in this shelter until the storm blew itself out and they were able to resume their journey. When they reached Georgetown, Sax said good-bye to his new friends. The rescued man was called Ray. He thanked them both with all his heart. "God had to have sent you", he said fervently. "It's the only answer to why you were there right then. How can I ever thank you for my life? May God bless you!"

Sax then made his way to Dick's little spread, eager to see him and Betsy.

They welcomed him with open arms. Dick was no longer using a crutch, Sax was happy to see. Betsy was so happy to see him that she threw her arms around him in a vigorous hug. He chuckled, a little embarrassed, as he had been staring at her in wonder, at her changed appearance in the blue muslin dress which emphasized her womanly curves. He couldn't get over how pretty she was.

"I'm so glad to see you," she bubbled. "I didn't know if you'd really come back or not."

Dick, too, had a wide smile, as he shook Sax's hand and patted him on the back. "Come," he said, "we'll help you take care of the horses and then we can have a nice visit."

Sax was soon sharing his impressions of Leadville and what he had learned about the Ice Palace. Then he told them about the adventure in the blizzard and about Ray being buried in the slide.

"How awful!" Betsy exclaimed. "You could have been killed!"

"It was like Ray said," he told her. "God had me there for a reason. And He took care of me and my partner."

The next few days were spent resting and catching up on what had been happening in their lives. Then it was time to say good-bye again. Betsy tried to put on a brave face, but she couldn't hide a few tears glistening in her eyes. She was afraid this might be a permanent farewell. "I know I shouldn't have," she thought, "but I fell in love with him. And he has said nothing to make me think he feels the same."

Father and daughter were both out to help him pack his gear on the spare horse and get ready to leave. Sax had a lump in his throat that he couldn't seem to swallow, as he looked at Betsy. He shook hands with Dick and told him how glad he was that he was back on his feet. Then he turned to Betsy and took both her hands in his, saying. "You don't know what this time has meant to me! Don't ever change! You're very special."

As he rode away she consoled herself," At least, he thinks I'm special, but that isn't enough!"

CHAPTER 20

The ride back to the valley of Charlie's ranch wasn't as pleasant as the one leaving had been. Not only was the weather colder, but Sax was having a bad feeling about having been gone so long. Even though Charlie had appeared in better health than he had been for some time, Sax knew that the frail old man had, at other times, seemed more robust and then lost strength equally as fast.

"I shouldn't have stayed so long," he berated himself," but I sure wanted to see Betsy again, too."

Nevertheless, he hurried as much as he could to reach the ranch and was relieved when it finally came into view. Before even going to the barn to unsaddle his horses, he leaped off his mount and dashed into the house. Soo Ling met him with his usual broad smile and sing-song words of greeting. Then his face grew sad as he said, "Chollee very sickee! He wait for Sax boy come home."

Sax hurried into Charlie's room, where the old man lay in bed, His slight form almost hidden by the covers. His breathing was labored, but his eyes lit up at the sight of Sax.

"Welcome home, Son!" He wheezed. "I sure missed you, and that's a fact."

"I'm sorry I was gone so long," Sax started to apologize. Charlie shook his head, saying, "Now, none of that! Sit down and tell me all about your adventures. You must have some good stories to tell me." He paused, looking at Sax, still bundled up in heavy coat.

"But that can wait 'til you get warmed up and fed. Now go on and get yourself taken care of. I'm not goin' anywhere for awhile!"

Reluctantly, the young man withdrew. He was shocked at just how frail and sick Charlie had grown. He had always been slight and rather stoop-shouldered, but he had also had a strong wiry strength about him. To see him bed-fast, pale and gasping for breath was almost more than Sax could put a brave face on.

However, he left the room, thinking to take care of his animals, but discovered that Soo Ling had already had his sons take care of that for him. So he took his outer wraps off and washed up for a warm, filling meal, set before him by the ever helpful Chinaman.

As soon as that was taken care of, he returned to Charlie's bedside. He drew up a chair for an extended visit. "Charlie," he began. "I hardly know where to start."

The old man smiled. "I've always found the beginning is usually a good place to start!"

So that's what Sax did, telling him about his enjoyment of the ride to the Georgetown area and how he had passed the time thinking about the stories that Charlie had previously told him. Then he explained how he had come across this girl who needed help, and her Dad, who was laid up with broken bones. Well, he couldn't just ride away, could he?

Charlie would insert a question now and then. After clarifying whatever it was, Sax would continue his tale. It took the better part of the afternoon to get everything told.

Soo Ling came in with some soup for Charlie, so Sax left to give him a break. He thought the old man was weaker than when he arrived, so was quite worried about him. Charlie had always been the father-figure in his life that his own father had never filled. He dreaded the thought of losing him.

After the evening meal, Sax went back to check on him again. Charlie reached for his hand and told him, "I have something to tell you while I am able. You have always been the son to me that I lost long ago. You don't know what that has meant to me all these years. I don't have anyone else, so I have made it legal that you are now the owner of this ranch. You helped me make it into a real ranch and you deserve it." He held up a hand weakly, when Sax started to protest.

"Don't argue. It's settled. I know, and you can see, that my time is very short now. I can tell that you have feelings for that Betsy girl. Don't let her get away! Bring her here to your home!"

Then he told Sax where the papers were that confirmed him as owner of the ranch, after which he fell into a fitful sleep. Sax continued to sit beside him, clutching the hand of the one who had meant so much to him. In the early morning hours, Charlie breathed his last, as Sax buried his face on Charlie's chest, sobbing.

Everyone on the ranch mourned Charlie's death. He had been a good and kind boss. Sax wondered about telling them that he was to be their boss now, but it was not necessary, as Charlie had already made his wishes known. Besides, they had all worked with Sax and Charlie together enough to know how things were between the two. Sax had worked at every part of the running of the outfit, enough to know how things needed to be done.

He went at his tasks with a vengeance, trying to work off his sorrow. Cattle had to be fed and repairs made to keep things shipshape before spring calving, planting, and other time consuming work started.

He thought of Betsy often, but had no idea when he would have a chance to go see her again. He thought of Charlie's words to him about not letting her get away, but didn't know what to do about it. He had never been interested in women before. At least, not in that way, and had no experience in courting one. Thinking about it frustrated him.

He knew how things needed to be done, but Charlie had always been the one that saw that they were. Knowing that the responsibility was now his bothered him. Although he had always had a good working relationship with all the men on the ranch, he felt uncomfortable at giving orders.

Finally, Fred Smith, the married foreman approached him, asking to speak to him privately.

"Sax, we all know that Charlie considered you his son, and we respect that, and we know that you worked as hard as he did building up this ranch. So quit acting like you're the new comer! You're the boss now and we all know it. Act like it!"

Sax thanked him and said he would do his best. However, when he needed to have certain jobs done, he still softened them by getting the man's opinion of the task first. As time passed, the old camaraderie returned. He also turned more frequently to Fred for his opinion on many matters. They became really good friends, and Sax was able to confide and turn to him when he was troubled. He found himself telling Fred about Betsy and how much he cared for her. "I think about her all the time and I really want to marry her, but I don't know if she feels the same, and I don't know anything about courtin' a woman. I never had feelings like this about anyone else."

"Well," Fred drawled, "you're shore not goin' to find out settin' up here thinkin' about her! Get on your horse and go show her how you feel. Buy her some candy or flowers or somethin', and ask her to go for dinner or a walk. Do somethin' besides settin' here makin' yourself miserable. Tell her how you feel. The girl can't read your mind!"

CHAPTER 21

One evening, Dick Jackson said to his daughter, "We need to talk, honey."

She looked at his serious face and said, "Whatever is it, Pop?"

"Well, you know it's been a rough winter, but the fact is we're just not gonna make it on this place. Expenses have been more than we can make. The fact is, we're broke. I'm gonna sell for whatever we can get and move into Georgetown. I can work at the Livery there and maybe you can work at a hotel or café. I know you like the ranch life, but it's just too hard."

Betsy put her arms around her father and hugged him. "It's alright. I know how hard it has been for you. We will do whatever we have to and I know things will get better."

Dick rode into town the next day and was able to make arrangements to sell the few livestock that were left. He put a notice in the paper for the sale of the property and searched for a cheap place to rent. Luckily, he found a small house that had just been vacated by someone heading back East.

He rode home feeling more optimistic than he had in a long time. The following few days were spent in packing their necessary belongings onto their old wagon. Then they hitched the team to the wagon, tying the saddle horses behind, and turned their backs on the little place that had been home.

Dick was hired at the Livery stable and went to work immediately. Betsy spent the next few days arranging their new living quarters. Then she went looking for work. After several inquiries, she found a position waiting tables at a hotel restraint, called "Finer Diner".

She found it lived up to its name and was a popular place for both locals and hotel guests. The work kept her mind from dwelling on Sax, and she and her father found a measure of contentment in their new life. Dick had found a buyer for the small ranch, as it had been priced so low that a young couple had been able to get it.

One day, as Betsy was serving a young man his meal, he spoke to her, after hearing her exchange words with another waitress. "Excuse me, miss, but I heard her call you Betsy. I don't suppose it's likely, but would you be Betsy Jackson?" "Why, yes, I am," she replied in surprise. "How would you know?"

"You see, I travelled to Georgetown with Sax Saxon some time ago, and he mentioned a girl by the name of Betsy Jackson…told me what a nice, pretty girl she was." He smiled at her; "I see he was right!"

She was so excited to meet someone who knew Sax. "You must be Bob Wilson then. He told us all about your close call and the fellow in the snow slide!" Betsy looked around, "Oh, I would like to talk more, but I have to get back to work," she exclaimed with a disappointed little frown. He nodded and said, "Later, then?" as she hurried off.

Bob watched her dark curls bounce as she disappeared through the kitchen door to collect another meal for a patron. "Yes, we'll definitely talk later," he said to himself.

When Betsy ended her shift and was walking toward their present home, Bob suddenly appeared beside her. Giving her a wide grin, he said, "I told you we'd talk later. Do you mind if I walk you home?"

She agreed and they fell into step together. She was eager to hear his version of the story told by Sax and he wanted to learn about her and how she was now in town instead of on a ranch. Their animated conversation soon had them at her door. Dick had just arrived also and was concerned to see his daughter with a stranger.

As he stepped through the door, Betsy exclaimed," Pop, you'll never guess who this is! It's Bob Wilson who came to Georgetown with Sax. Remember how they were in that blizzard together?"

Relaxing upon hearing this, Dick extended his hand and grasped the young man's. "A friend of Sax is a friend of mine," he said. "Come in and stay for supper. We'll have a nice visit."

Bob was surprised that they had heard nothing from Sax since he left them. He definitely had got the impression the young man had feelings for this girl. And the way Betsy had lit up when talking about Sax, he thought she must feel the same about him.

"You mean he hasn't even written to you!" he exclaimed. "I thought sure he would keep in touch with you."

Betsy replied wistfully, "I thought so, too, but he did say he wasn't much good at writing, and I remember he had a hard time even sending a note to his friend, Charlie, so he wouldn't worry about him before he went to Leadville. Then, when he came back from there, he was anxious to get home because he said he was concerned about Charlie."

They had a very pleasant evening and Bob left with a standing invitation to come by anytime, which he took advantage of, and became a frequent visitor.

He liked and enjoyed Dick's company, but his main attraction was Betsy. She seemed prettier and more desirable every time he saw her.

Soon he was renting a rig and coming by to take her for an evening ride or going for a stroll to an ice cream parlor for a treat. He had the feeling that Sax had given up on any chance with Betsy so he figured he wasn't poaching on another man's girl.

Betsy really liked this young man and enjoyed her time with him, but he didn't excite her as Sax had, or make her heart thump wildly or her knees feel all trembly. She didn't love him, but considered him a good friend.

Bob, on the other hand, was falling more in love with her each time he was with her. He thought about her all the time. At least she was never far from his thoughts. He definitely planned to ask her to marry him.

CHAPTER 22

After Sax thought over what Fred had said to him, he knew his friend was right. How could Betsy know how he felt if he stayed here and didn't make any effort to see her?

He found his friend and foreman and told him," You're right, Fred. I've been like they say those ostriches are…burying my head in the sand! You look after the place here. I'm going to see if I have a chance with Betsy!"

He lost no time in packing a few belongings and saddling his sleek black horse. Giving a few words of farewell to those he saw and especially to his old friend, Soo Ling, he rode away.

This was not the leisurely journey that his first trip to Georgetown had been. He was in a hurry and made as good time as he could. He was surprised when he rode into the little ranch and saw a strange young man working around the yard. Swinging down from his horse, he inquired, "Is Dick or Betsy around?"

The stranger smiled and replied, "No, I'm the new owner here…Samuels is my name. You must be a friend of the guy I bought it from."

Sax shook the man's hand, saying, "I didn't know they had sold it. Do you know where they went? I came quite a way to see them."

"I don't really know. I only had dealings in regard to the property," he responded. "But I think they might still be in Georgetown."

Sax thanked the young man as he remounted and then rode out of the yard, resuming the trip to Georgetown and his search for the Jackson's. He thought he had better get a place to stay first, before starting his search. He arranged a room in a hotel for himself and then went to find a livery barn for his horse. Georgetown was large enough to have more than one, so he was not fortunate enough to go to the one where Dick Jackson worked.

In the next couple of days, he inquired at various hotels and rooming houses about the Jackson's, with no results. Then he considered, since they had a team of horses, wouldn't they need a place for them to stay? Unless, of course, they had sold them, as they had the ranch.

Nevertheless, Sax started his search for other livery stables. On his third try, he found his answer in none other than Dick, himself. They had a joyful reunion, thumping each other on the back and grinning broadly.

"It's almost time for me to go home," Dick said, "and you have to come with me. Betsy will be so happy to see you. We couldn't help worryin' some about you since we never heard a word since you left."

"I'm sorry about that," Sax responded. "I'm having second thoughts about a lot of things lately… especially that!"

This turned to embarrassment at the way she had reacted, and her face was like a blossomed, rosy red.

Sax was equally struck silent as he gazed at the lovely girl, adorned in a long, stylish, green dress; her hair, a mass of curls atop her head. He thought of the way she looked when he had first seen her; clad in overalls, with a smudge on her cheek, and he had first thought her to be a boy. He shook his head to clear that vision from his mind before he could speak.

"Betsy, it's so good to see you. I went to the ranch first and found new people there. I've been looking ever since, trying to find you both." He included both in the statement, but his eyes never left Betsy.

The evening was spent filling each other in on the events of the past months. They expressed their sympathy when they learned of Charlie's death, knowing how much the old man had meant to Sax. He, in turn, told them how sorry they had to sell their little ranch, but they surprised him by saying, "It was really a blessing! The place was more than we could handle and we were barely getting by. Since then, we have both been working and making a little money and what we got for the place has helped out, too. We're better off than we were and not working near as hard!"

Sax told them that his circumstances had changed, too, as he was now the owner of the ranch that Charlie had started years ago, and it was doing quite well, with plenty of capable help.

As the evening wore on, he was asked, "Where are you staying? We would ask you to stay with us, but this place is quite small, as you can see."

Sax reassured them, "I am at a hotel for a few more days, at least, but I understand and appreciate the intent of your offer. Now, I had better leave and let you both get some rest, since you are both working."

They agreed, but insisted he come for supper the following evening. Sax spent the time before sleep claimed him, rejoicing that he had found his friends and hoping he would have a chance to spend some time alone with Betsy.

The following day, he eagerly waited for the time to pass so he could join them again. He even went early to the livery so he could talk to Dick and walk home with him when he left. He eagerly waited for a sight of Betsy, and was rewarded when she threw open the door and said. "Sax, you'll never guess who is here! I forgot to tell you last night. It's your old friend, Bob Wilson."

At that moment, Bob stepped into sight, smiling broadly and clasped Sax's hand. "You're a sight for sore eyes, old buddy! It's mighty good to see you."

Sax's astonishment gave way to the pleasure of seeing his old friend, and he was eager to hear how he had met the Jackson's. This evening, too, was filled with lively conversation as various stories were related.

Before the evening came to a close, though, Sax couldn't help but notice the way Bob's eyes were constantly following Betsy. He recognized the look because he found himself doing the same. He glanced at Betsy to see if she was favoring Bob with any returning loving looks, but couldn't tell if she was. The evening ended with laughter and good fellowship from all.

The next few days followed the same pattern, but to Sax's frustration, he never had a moment alone with Betsy. Every evening Bob also showed up and often made remarks such as, "When are you going to have time for another buggy ride, Betsy?" Or, "Would you like to try a sundae next time instead of plain ice cream?"

One evening he came with a rented buggy, suggesting that Betsy go for a ride. Feeling guilty at going, but aware that Bob had rented the rig just for her, she agreed, but said, "Surely Sax can come with us."

He, however, quickly refused. "I have to be getting back home. I stayed away too long."

Dick, who was watching this little tableau, saw the sadness in Sax's eyes, and felt sure that his reference to staying away too long was about something other than the ranch. He felt sure that Sax loved his daughter and had been to shy to let her know. Bob's obvious wooing of Betsy was also obvious, but Dick didn't want to interfere, even though he thought her feelings had always been strongest for Sax.

Sax, however, left the Jacksons that night with a heavy heart. "I wanted to tell Betsy how I feel about her…that I wanted her for my wife, but how can I now? Bob is surely in love with her, too, and he's had all this time to win her. And, dang it all, anyway! He is my friend. How can I interfere now, after all this time? He's a good man and will make her a good husband."

Sadly, he made preparations to leave. The following morning, before Dick or Betsy had left for their respective jobs; he rode to their little house and told them good-bye. He turned away quickly and didn't see the shock and tears come to Betsy's expressive brown eyes. He didn't see Dick wrap his arms around her to comfort her as Sax left her a second time without telling her of his love.

As much as Sax had always loved being out in these mountains and eagerly watched for the wildlife along the way, this time he scarcely noticed his surroundings. He hurried homeward as fast as he had left earlier, and with an aching heart.

Fred and the ranch crew had expected him to come home with a bride, so were surprised at his somber expression as he dismounted from his horse. The others turned away after a quick "Glad you're back, Boss," but Fred lingered and, putting a hand on Sax's shoulder, asked, "What happened, son?"

Ducking his head and tensing his jaw, He mumbled, "I just waited too long." Then, turning away, he strode quickly for the house.

CHAPTER 23

In Georgetown, Bob Wilson found Betsy quieter and less lighthearted than usual. In an attempt to cheer her up, he was more attentive than ever, telling her funny stories he had heard, going for walks or rides and anything he could think of to win her smiles. One evening as they were returning from a walk, he took her hand and stopped before entering the house.

"Betsy, we have been seeing each other for quite some time now. You must know how I feel about you! I love you and want you to be my wife. Will you marry me?"

She shouldn't have been surprised, but she was. She had accepted him first, as a friend of Sax's; then as a dear friend of her own and her Pop's. Somehow, she just hadn't thought of him in a romantic way, probably because the only one she had considered in that light was Sax. She was still grieving over that situation.

She looked at Bob sadly. "I am so sorry! I really didn't mean to give you the wrong impression, Bob. I just think of you as a dear friend and I don't mean to hurt you, but I just can't marry you."

He swallowed his disappointment and forced a smile. "It's alright. I guess I always knew that you had eyes only for Sax, but when he left again, I thought I had a chance."

They soon said good night and he turned away and walked into the night.

Dick was aware that something had upset his daughter, so she explained what had happened. He told her, "You know Bob is a good man, Betsy He could make you a good husband."

"No, Pop, it wouldn't be fair to him or me…not knowing how I feel about Sax," she replied, with tears running down her cheeks. She turned and ran to her room, shutting the door firmly behind her.

Bob was thinking deeply, long into the night, after leaving Betsy. He remembered how Sax had told him about Betsy during their time traveling together; how he described her in vivid detail and couldn't say enough about her goodness and sweetness. He remembered how, during his last time in Georgetown, he couldn't keep his eyes from watching her every move. *Why in tarnation had he never told Betsy how he felt?* he thought to himself.

Maybe because he saw that I was courtin' her, Bob thought. It would be like him to back off for a friend. Well, maybe I can do the same for him, he said to himself.

The first thing in the morning, he hunted writing materials and started a letter.

Sax had been quieter than usual since being back at the ranch, but seemed to go out of his way to find more work to keep every hour busy, except when eating or sleeping, and he seemed to do less of both.

He groomed horses that were already sleek and shiny and checked any horseshoes that needed replaced. He checked and rechecked for things needing repaired. He rode fence lines, looking for any breaks; anything to keep occupied.

Fred watched him unobtrusively, with a worried frown. He told his wife, "The boss is losing weight… not eating right and workin' harder than two men. I'm worried about him."

She replied, "So am I! He even was out putting fence around my garden; saying he thought it would help by keeping rabbits and critters out. I've always taken care of my own garden!" She said this, a bit snappish, with a self-righteous shake of her head.

Fred threw an arm across her shoulder, replying in a soft voice, "It just goes to show that he's not himself these days."

Even Soo Ling couldn't tempt his appetite with his good cooking and special tidbits. Sax, who was usually so considerate and thoughtful of everyone, seemed unaware that he had everyone on the ranch concerned and keeping a watchful eye on him.

One day Fred had gone into the nearest town for supplies and to pick up any mail for his family or the ranch crew. He was surprised to get a letter for Sax because he could only remember one or two for him in all the years he had been there.

Sax was equally amazed when he was handed the letter. He saw that it was from Bob Wilson. Opening it, he read, "Sax, old buddy, I'm going to do you a favor and tell you to swallow your pride and hightail it back to Georgetown as fast as you can. You're breaking Betsy's heart. She won't marry me. She loves you, you silly ass. Open you're stupid mouth and tell her you feel the same. By the way, I'd be honored to be best man." Bob.

Sax had to read it several times before it really sank in, but when it did, he gave a rebel yell and, tossing his hat in the air in exuberance, ran and gave Fred a hug, telling him," Saddle my horse; I'm going back to Georgetown and this time I'm not comin' back alone!"

CHAPTER 24

S ax rode the familiar trail, which he had crossed a few weeks before, in a much better frame of mind. However, he couldn't help wondering if Bob was completely sure of what he'd told him about Betsy's feelings. He knew only that he was determined to find out for himself and tell her his true feelings.

When Dick opened the door to a knock, he was surprised to see Sax standing there, but grabbed him in a hug and pulled him inside.

"It's shore good to see you back, Son, but if you'll excuse me for sayin' it, you look like death warmed over! Have you been sick?"

"Only heart sick," Sax said, "but I hope to remedy that," He smiled and asked," Is Betsy still at work?"

"No, she's runnin' an errand, but should be here any time now. Sit down and have some coffee and tell me what's goin' on with you two? She looks about as bad as you do these days, and won't tell me anything except she won't marry Bob."

"I'm sorry to hear that…I mean I'm glad she's not marryin' Bob, but sorry she's poorly. I want to marry her, myself. That's why I came back, hoping she would agree."

Dick grinned broadly, saying. "It's about time you two came to your senses! I knew a long time ago how you felt about each other, even if you didn't seem to."

They both turned as the door opened and Betsy entered. She stopped, in shock, as she saw Sax. He noticed at once that Dick was right. She looked thinner and paler than when he had last seen her. She, in turn, was noticing his gaunt frame, that seemed to have somehow shrunk.

He moved first, going to her and taking the package from her arms, setting it on the table, then turning back and taking her hands in his.

"Betsy, I've missed you so much, I can't even explain it! I thought you and Bob were getting married and somethin' inside of me just up and died. I was miserable and I made everyone around me miserable! Then Bob sent me a letter, sayin' you didn't marry him and callin' me all kinds of a fool! So I high-tailed it back as soon as I could. Is there a chance that you could…will, marry me? I love you more than I ever thought I could love someone."

Betsy threw her arms around his neck. "Oh, Sax. I thought I was the only one who felt that way. I love you…have for so long! Bob was only a friend and I like him, but mainly because he was a friend of yours.

I thought it was hopeless, but yes, yes, I would love to marry you!"

They had completely forgotten Dick was taking this all in with a delighted grin on his face. He cleared his throat to get their attention, saying, "Well, you didn't ask my permission, but the answer is yes! I give my blessing to this wedding."

Betsy laughed and kissed her father's cheek. "Thanks, Pop, but I already knew you would!"

"Well," Dick replied, "there's a lot to talk about this evening. You know, all the when's and wherefores."

That is exactly how they did spend the evening. They both agreed that they wanted to be married as soon as possible. Sax told them that he needed to see Bob, as he had offered to be his best man. He also told them that he didn't want to be away from the ranch much longer, as he felt he had neglected it in the past. He thought he owed Charlie better.

"You know, Dick, you're welcome to come to the ranch, too. We can always use another hand around the place."

"Thanks, son, I know you mean it, but I like workin' at the Livery, and I wasn't a very good rancher, so I think I'll stay right here. Betsy, on the other hand, loved the ranch, in spite of all the hard work. I know she will do real well with you, and I'm real happy for you both."

As Sax left that evening for a hotel room, He gathered Betsy in his arms and gave her his first passionate kiss, whispering that he could hardly wait for their wedding.

The following day, Betsy told her employer at the Finer Diner that she was getting married and would be leaving. She had made friends of all the other employees, as well as her employer, who suggested they use one of their banquet rooms for her wedding. She was told if it could be done after their serving hours, all of them would attend. She was so touched by this offer; she couldn't prevent a few tears.

Sax spent the day looking up Bob, who was happy to see him. "I'm glad you took my advice," he told Sax. "You are a lucky man! Betsy is a wonderful woman, but I guess I knew all along how she felt about you, but since you never did anything about it, I hoped. Maybe some day I'll find another girl like her, if I'm as lucky as you!"

He agreed to be best man for Sax. The other necessities had to be arranged; the time, the ring, the preacher, clothes to be wed in, and a horse for Betsy to ride on the return trip. Some of the trails were not for a buggy.

Soon, all these details had been taken care of and it was time for the big event. Betsy's friends at the diner had decorated the banquet room with flowers and colorful ribbons. A makeshift altar had been made with a table, covered in white cloth, and a huge bouquet of flowers in the center. Tables had been moved to the sides of the room and chairs arranged in rows, with an aisle between, leading to the altar.

The preacher, Sax and Bob waited there for Dick to escort his daughter down the makeshift aisle. Betsy looked lovely in a powder blue dress with white collar and trim. Her dark curls were tied back from her face with a white ribbon.

Sax couldn't take his eyes off her. She felt much the same, gazing at the tall, young man with the most handsome features and bluest eyes that she was sure she had ever seen.

The preacher went through his ritual and Bob handed Sax the ring to slip on Betsy's finger. The preacher proclaimed them man and wife and Sax took possession of his new bride with a lingering kiss.

As a final surprise for the bride and groom, her former employer brought forth a beautiful wedding cake to serve to the guests. Betsy thought it was the most beautiful wedding she had ever dreamed of. Sax had thought it would just be the four of them; him, Betsy Bob and Dick, and the preacher, of course. But to his surprise, there were more than a dozen friends of Betsy and Dick there to celebrate and wish them well.

Their first night was spent in the hotel where they were finally able to caress and make love to their mutual delight. Even their trip home was like a magic carpet ride, as far as they were concerned. They delighted in every touch or smile and learned little things about each other that they had not known before.

When they arrived at the ranch, it was another celebration all over. Soo Ling and the women of the place went to great lengths to welcome Betsy with fancy meals and heart felt warmth. They were all happy to have Sax back in his usual good humor and were genuinely happy that he had found the bride of his choice. Betsy settled in happily. She loved the ranch and liked all the people on it. "I never thought I could be this happy!" she told Sax. He agreed with her wholeheartedly.

One day he took her for a ride out toward some cliffs where he had often watched eagles soaring and building their nest on the craggy ridges. As he pointed them out to her, he told her how his mother had once told him, "We are going where the eagles soar."

"I am finally with them," he said. "You brought me home. I'm soaring with the eagles!"